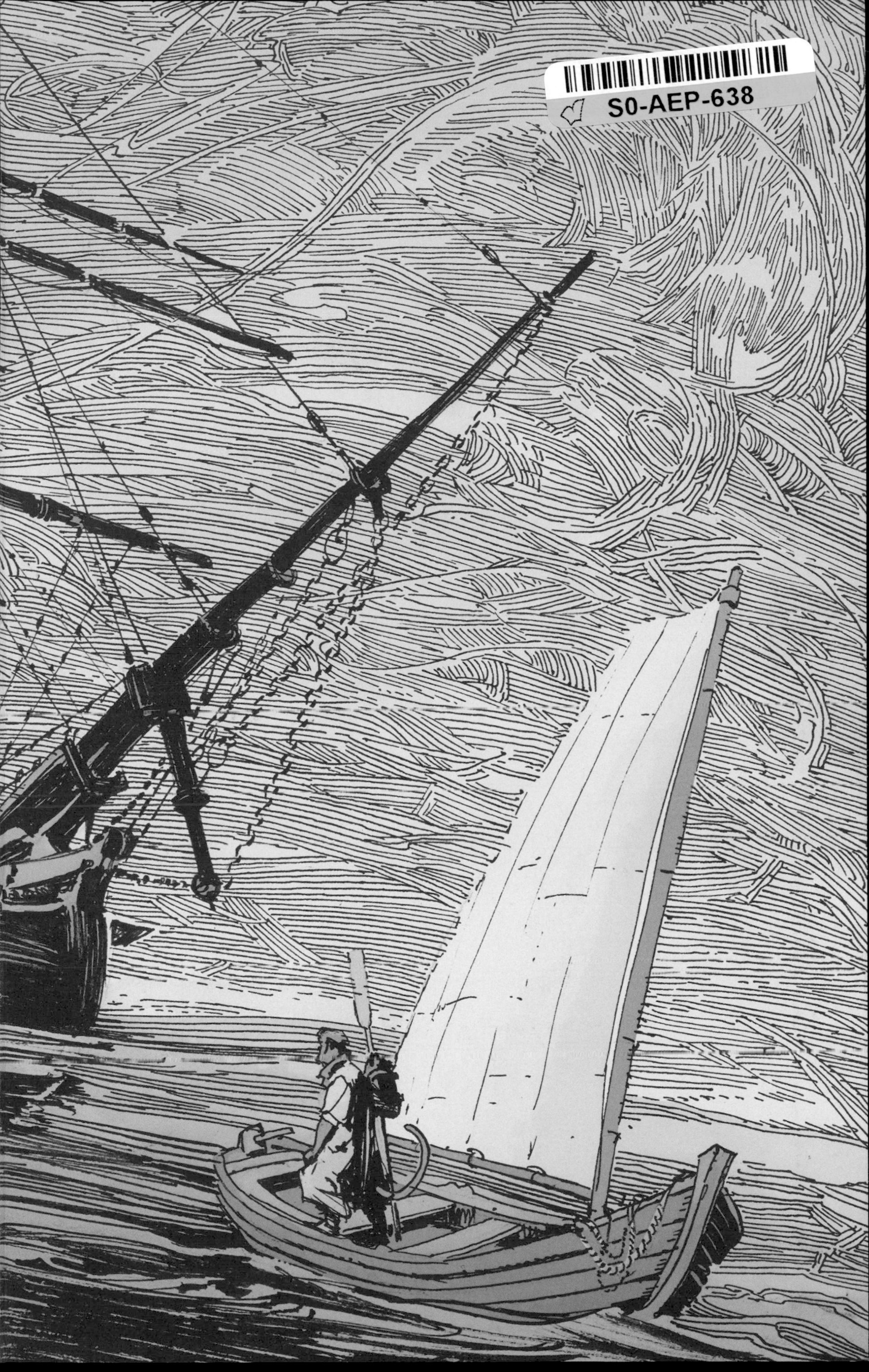

HELLBOY ™

INTO THE SILENT SEA

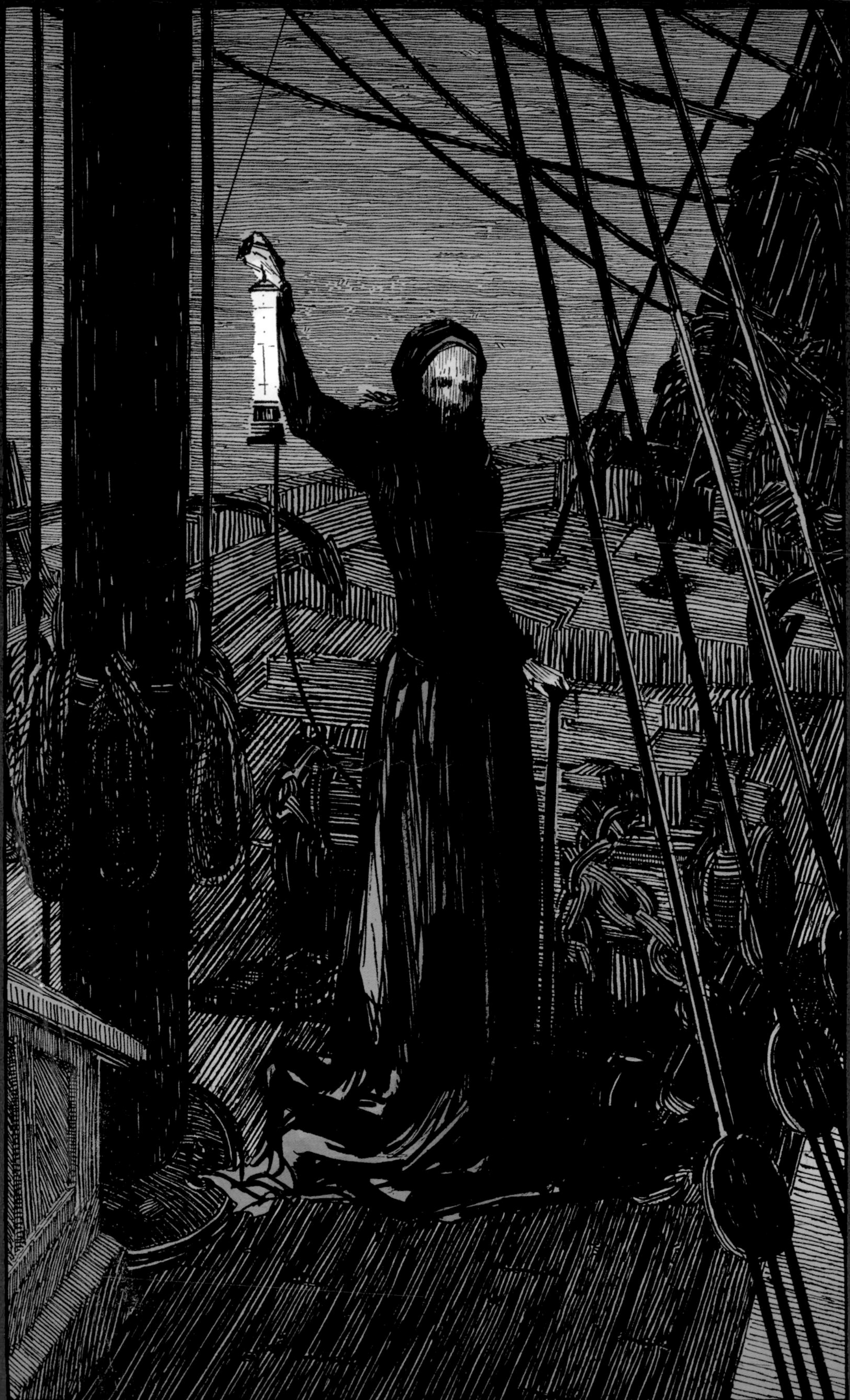

HELLBOY

INTO THE SILENT SEA

Story by
MIKE MIGNOLA & GARY GIANNI

Art by
GARY GIANNI

Colors by
DAVE STEWART

Letters by
CLEM ROBINS

✠

Cover art by
MIKE MIGNOLA *with* DAVE STEWART

Publisher
MIKE RICHARDSON

Editor
SCOTT ALLIE

Assistant Editor
KATII O'BRIEN

Collection Designers
MIKE MIGNOLA & CARY GRAZZINI

Digital Art Technician
CHRISTINA McKENZIE

DARK HORSE BOOKS

Published by Dark Horse Books
A division of Dark Horse Comics, Inc.
10956 SE Main Street
Milwaukie, OR 97222

Advertising Sales (503) 905-2237
International Licensing (503) 905-2377
Comic Shop Locator Service (888) 266-4226

DarkHorse.com
Facebook.com/DarkHorseComics
Twitter.com/DarkHorseComics

First edition: April 2017
ISBN 978-1-50670-143-1

HELLBOY: INTO THE SILENT SEA

Library of Congress Cataloging-in-Publication Data

Names: Mignola, Michael, author, artist. | Gianni, Gary, author, artist. |
Robins, Clem, 1955- letterer. | Stewart, Dave, colourist, artist.
Title: Hellboy, Into the silent sea / story by Mike Mignola and Gary Gianni ;
art by Gary Gianni ; colors by Dave Stewart ; letters by Clem Robins ;
cover art by Mike Mignola with Dave Stewart.
Other titles: Into the silent sea
Description: First edition. | Milwaukie, OR : Dark Horse Books, 2017.
Identifiers: LCCN 2016049406 | ISBN 9781506701431 (hardback)
Subjects: LCSH: Comic books, strips, etc. | BISAC: COMICS & GRAPHIC NOVELS /
Horror. | COMICS & GRAPHIC NOVELS / Fantasy. | FICTION / Sea Stories.
Classification: LCC PN6727.M53 H49 2017 | DDC 741.5/973--dc23
LC record available at https://lccn.loc.gov/2016049406

1 3 5 7 9 10 8 6 4 2

Printed in China

For John Huston, Ray Bradbury,
and Gregory Peck—and Herman Melville,
because they couldn't have done it without him.
And, of course, for William Hope Hodgson.
Mike Mignola

For Tom Gianni and Jack Kirby.
Gary Gianni

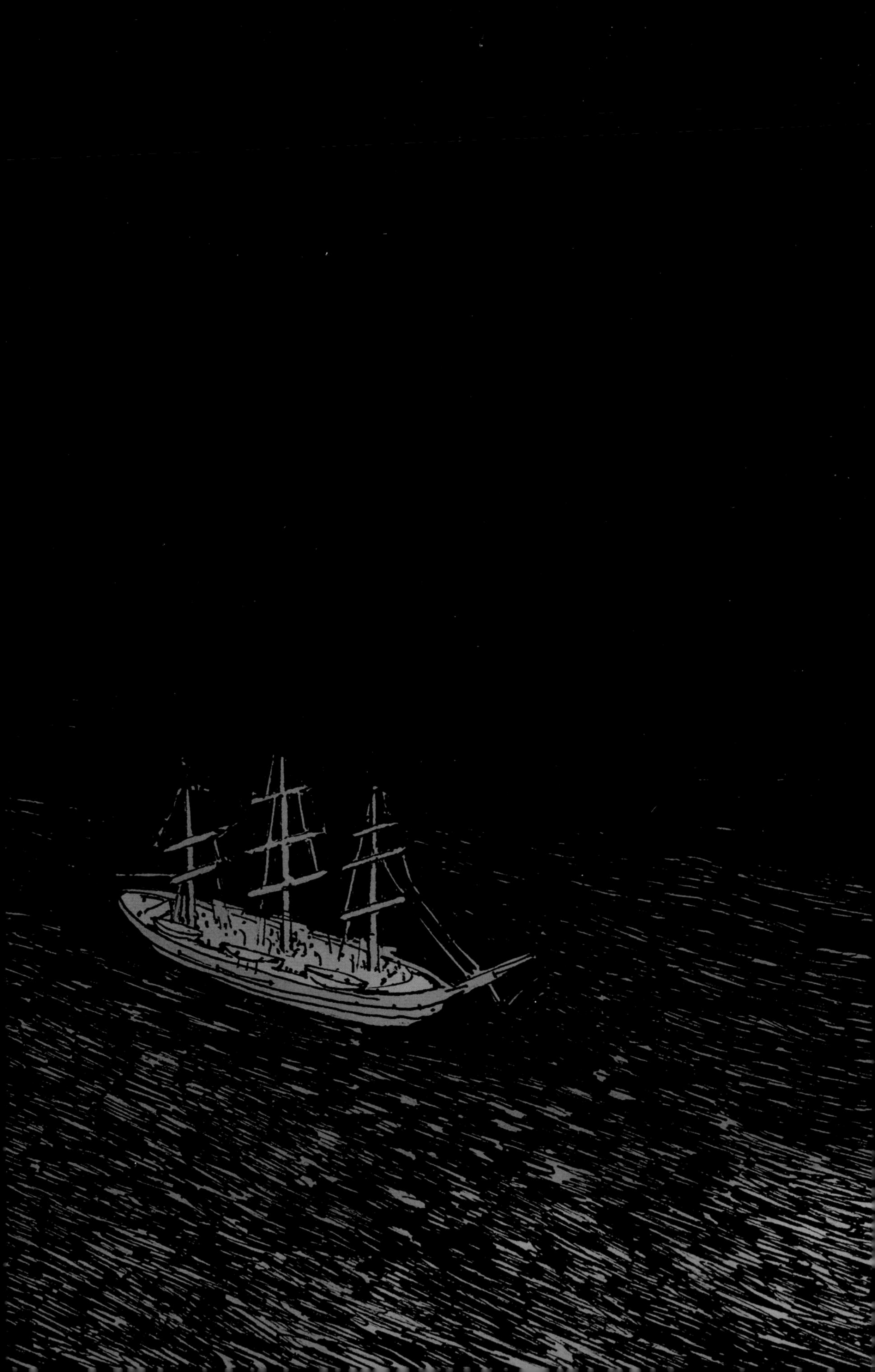

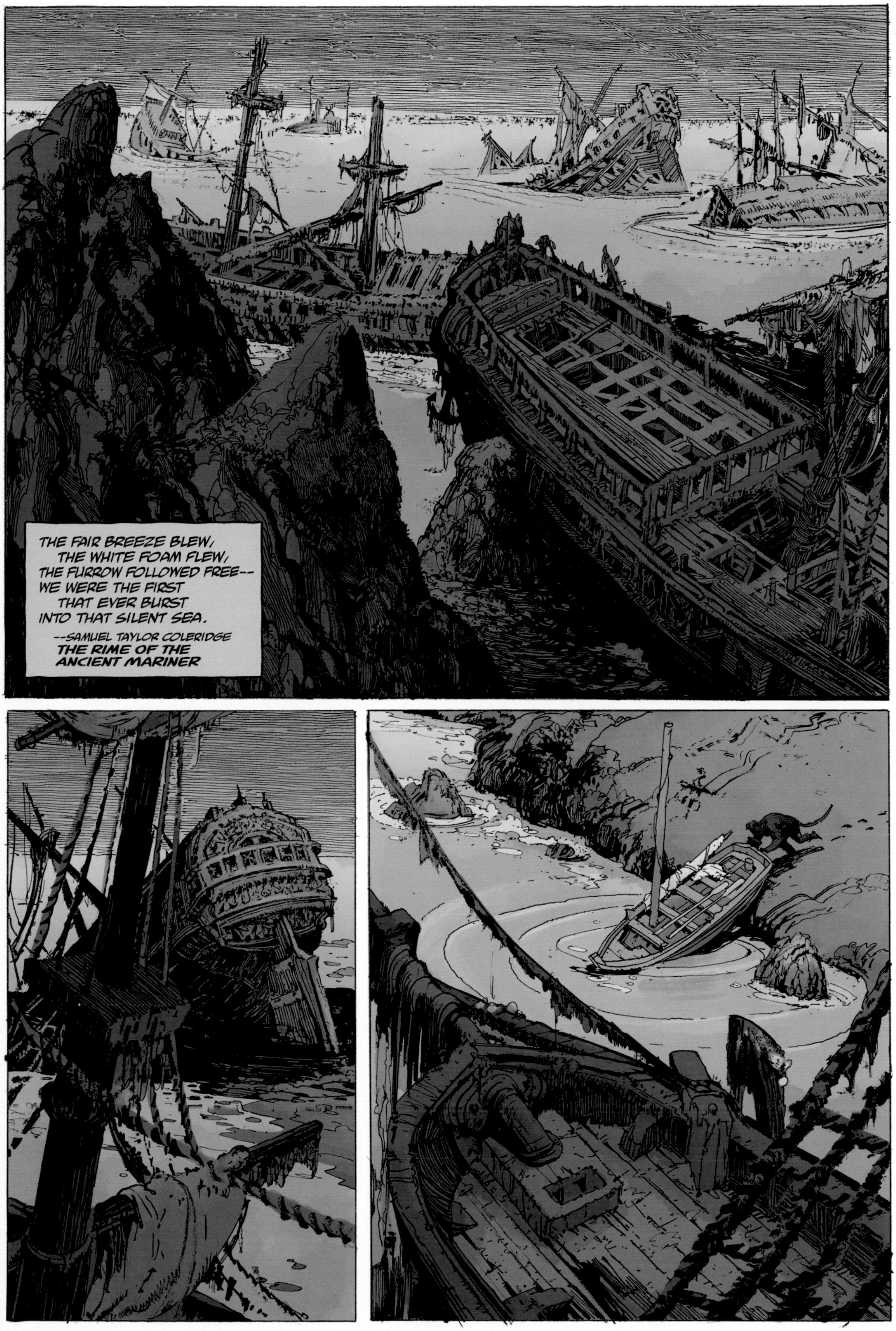
THE FAIR BREEZE BLEW,
THE WHITE FOAM FLEW,
THE FURROW FOLLOWED FREE--
WE WERE THE FIRST
THAT EVER BURST
INTO THAT SILENT SEA.
--SAMUEL TAYLOR COLERIDGE
THE RIME OF THE
ANCIENT MARINER

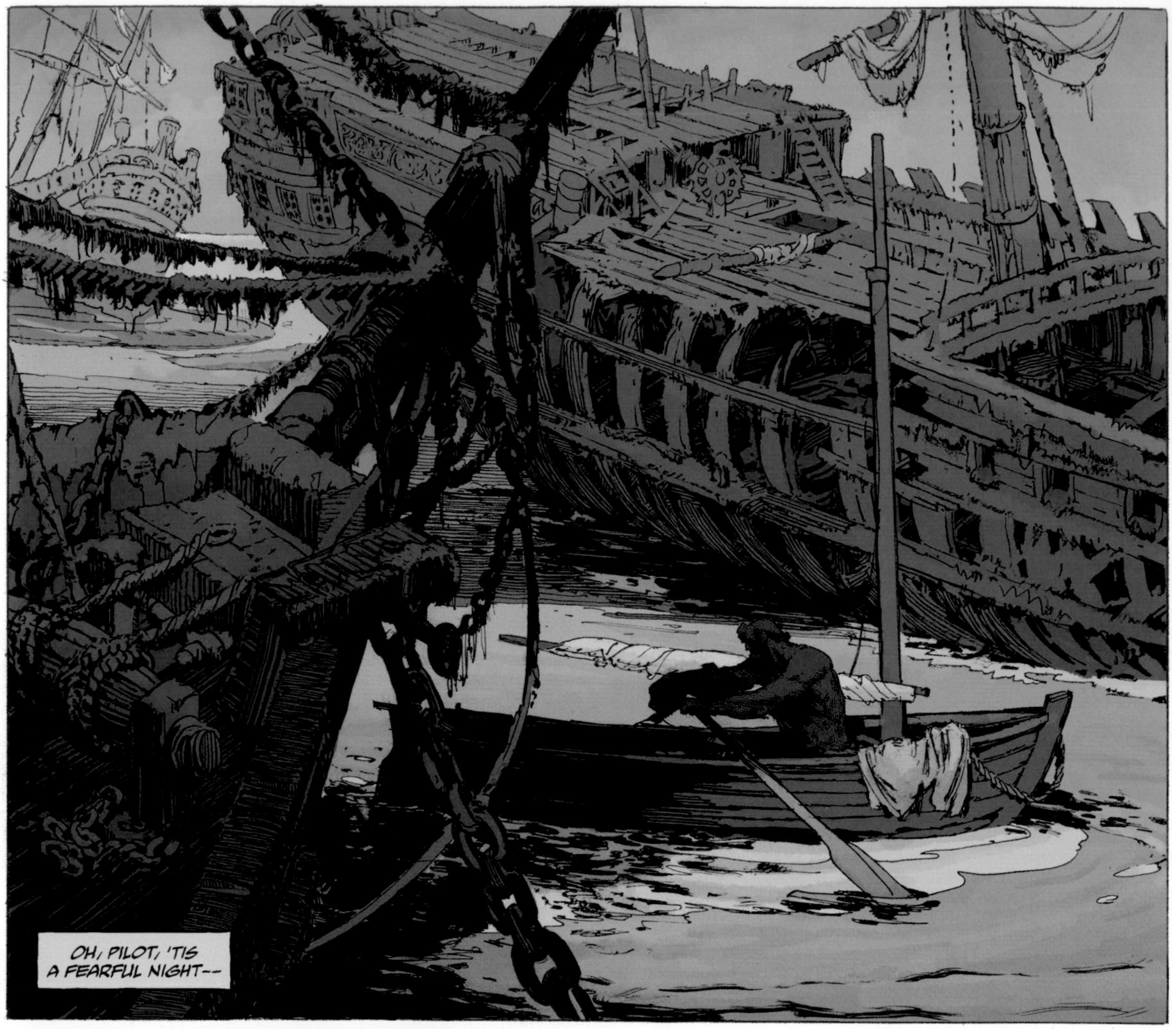
OH, PILOT, 'TIS
A FEARFUL NIGHT--

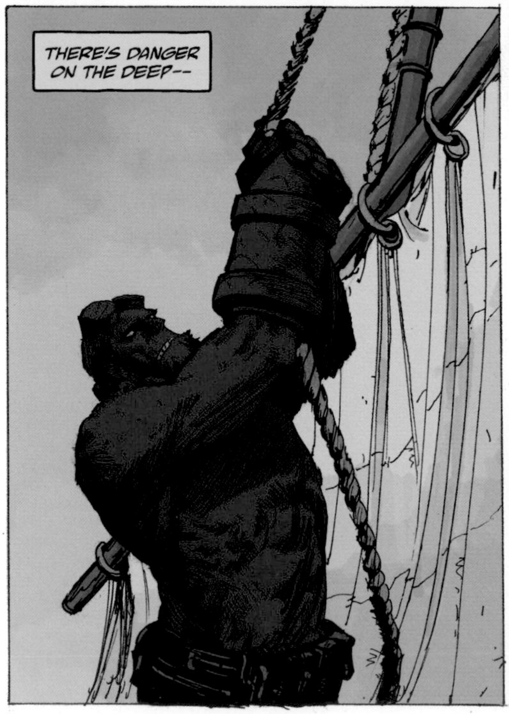
THERE'S DANGER
ON THE DEEP--

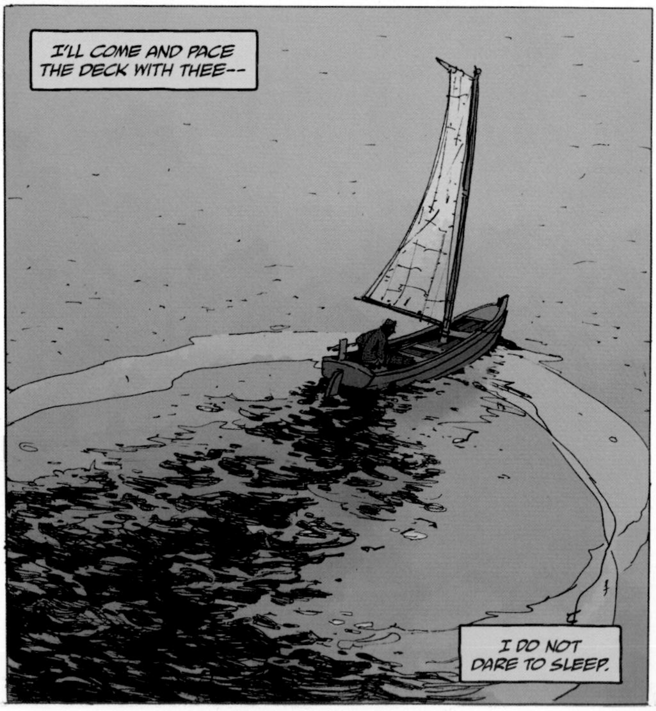
I'LL COME AND PACE
THE DECK WITH THEE--
I DO NOT
DARE TO SLEEP.

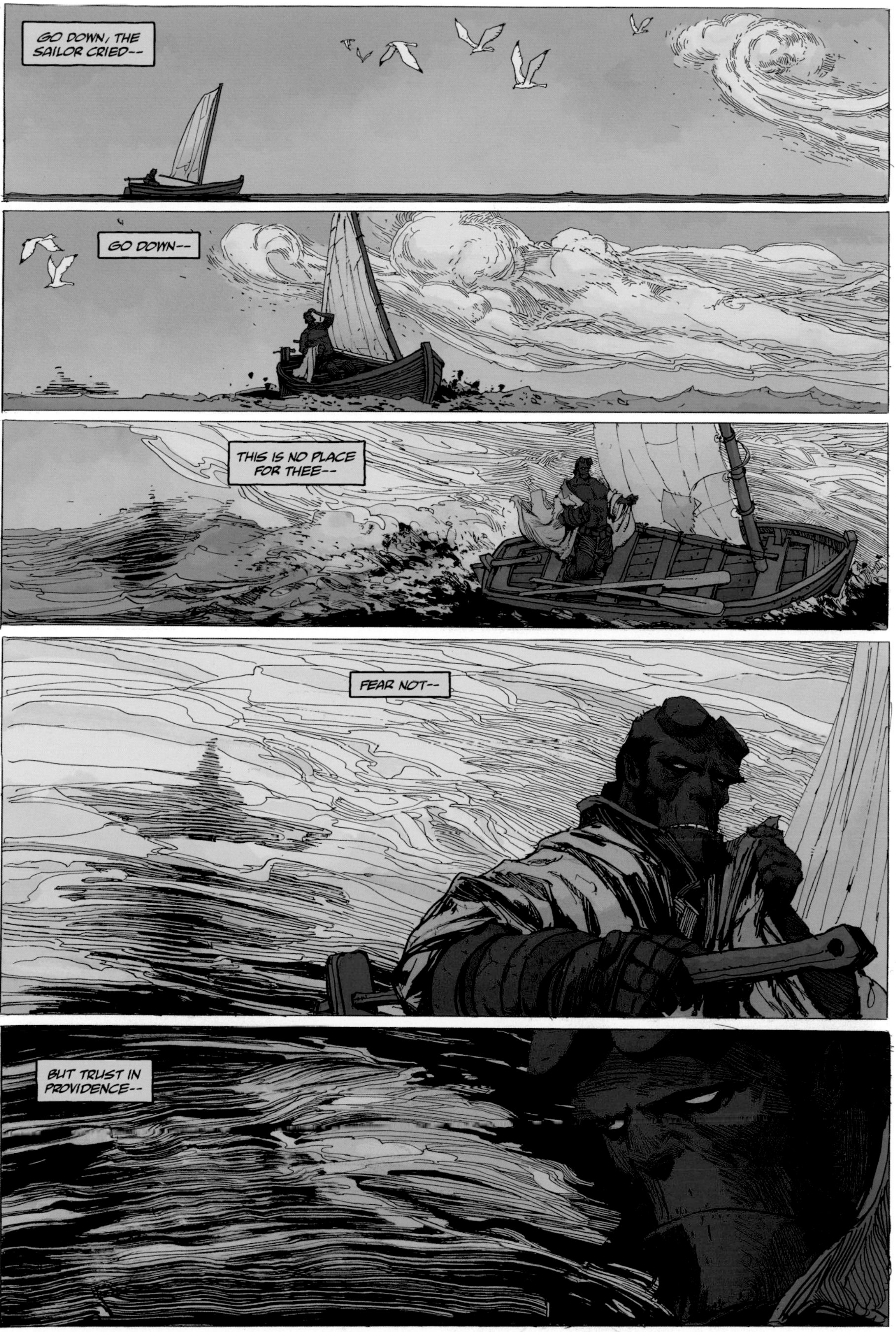
GO DOWN, THE SAILOR CRIED--
GO DOWN--
THIS IS NO PLACE FOR THEE--
FEAR NOT--
BUT TRUST IN PROVIDENCE--

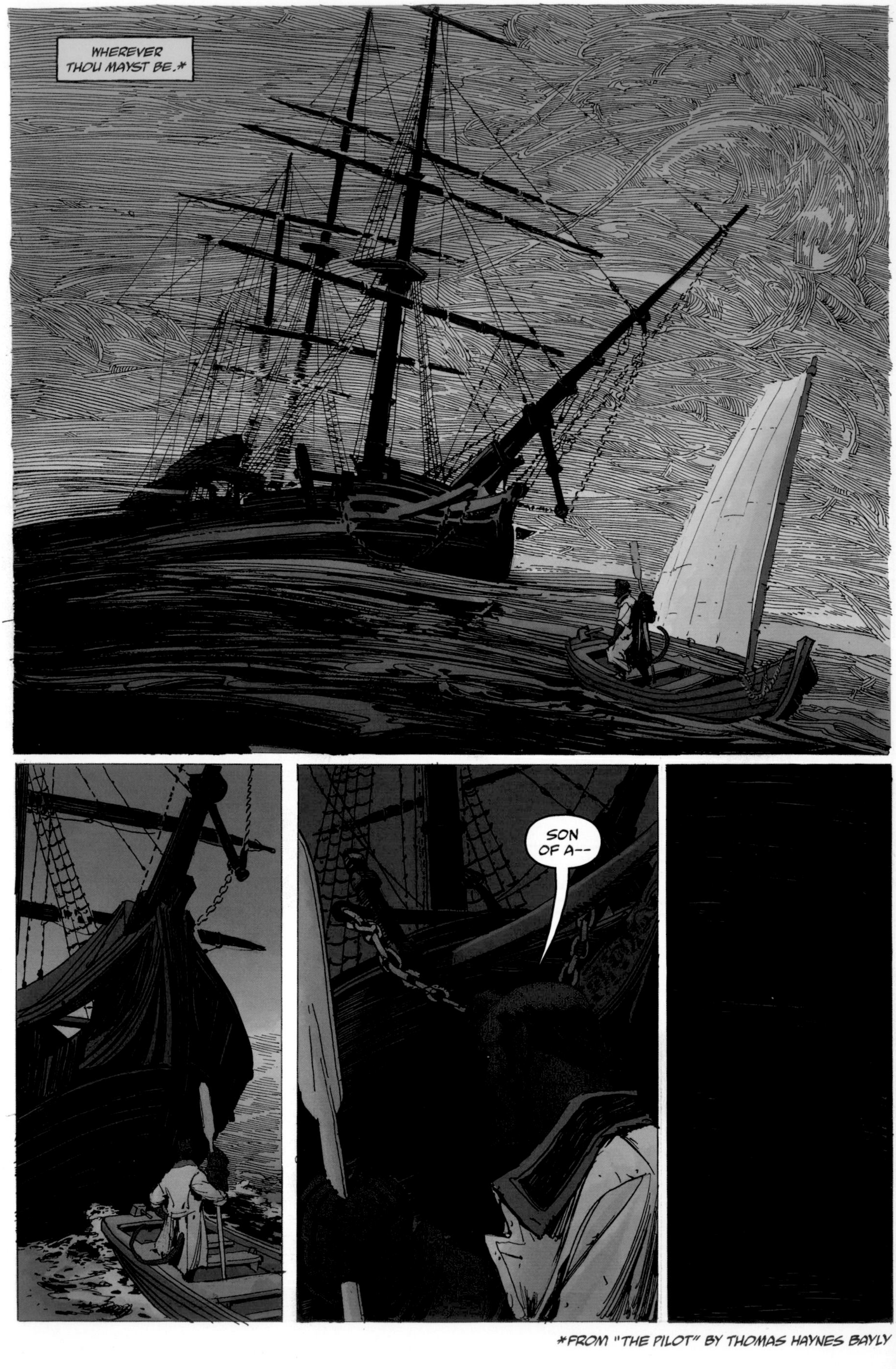
WHEREVER THOU MAYST BE.*
SON OF A--

*FROM "THE PILOT" BY THOMAS HAYNES BAYLY

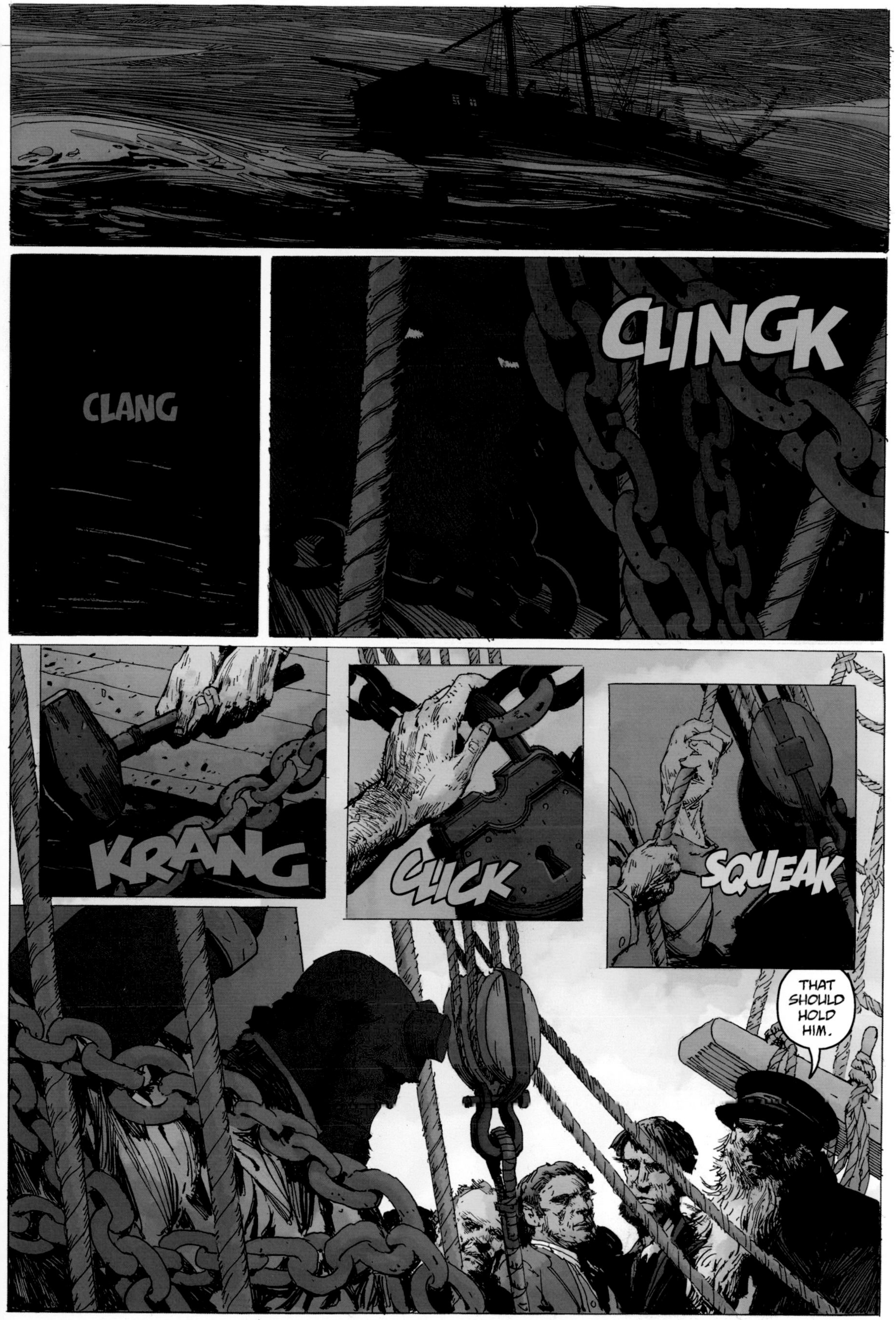
CLANG
CLINGK
KRANG
CLICK
SQUEAK
THAT SHOULD HOLD HIM.

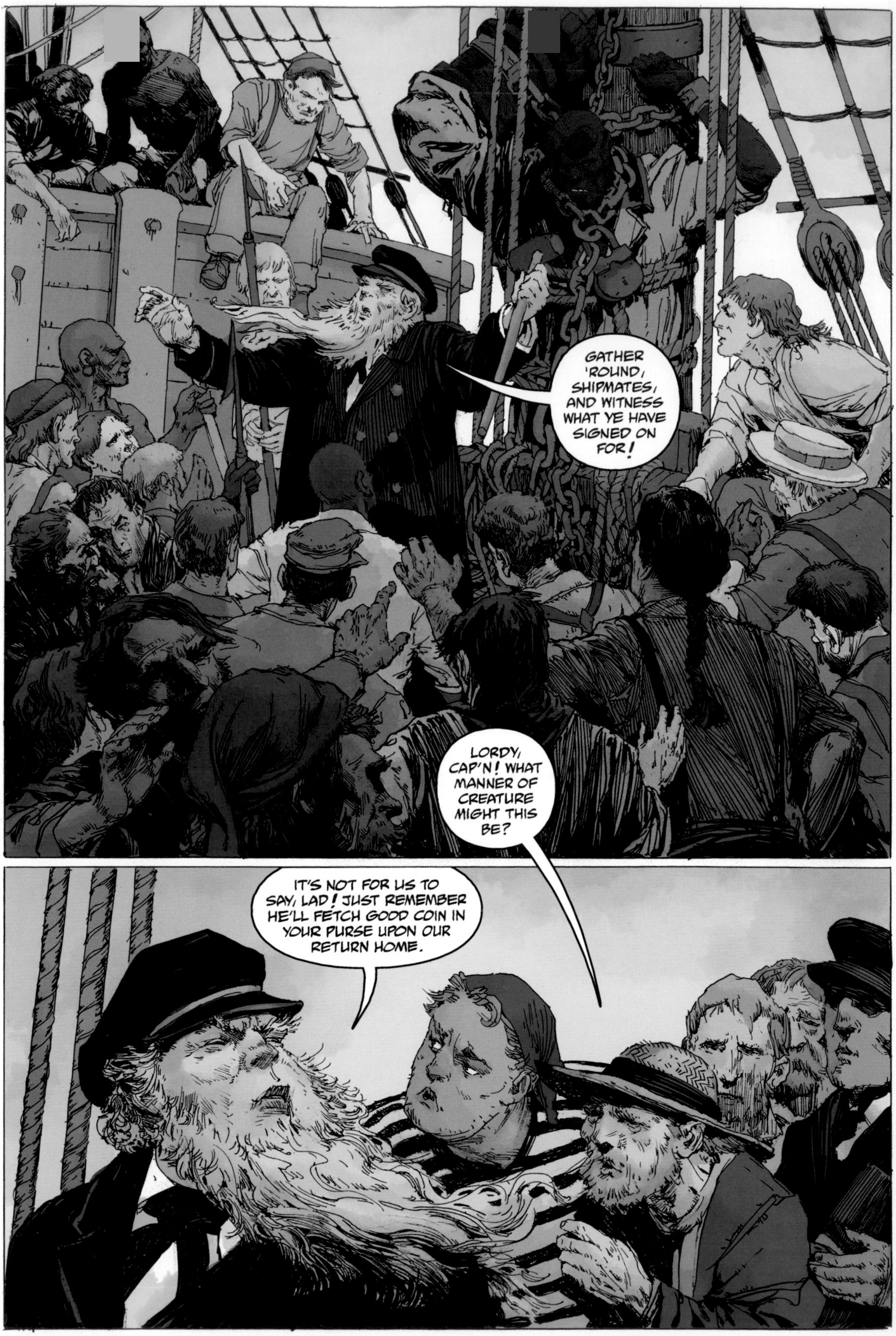
GATHER 'ROUND, SHIPMATES, AND WITNESS WHAT YE HAVE SIGNED ON FOR!
LORDY, CAP'N! WHAT MANNER OF CREATURE MIGHT THIS BE?
IT'S NOT FOR US TO SAY, LAD! JUST REMEMBER HE'LL FETCH GOOD COIN IN YOUR PURSE UPON OUR RETURN HOME.

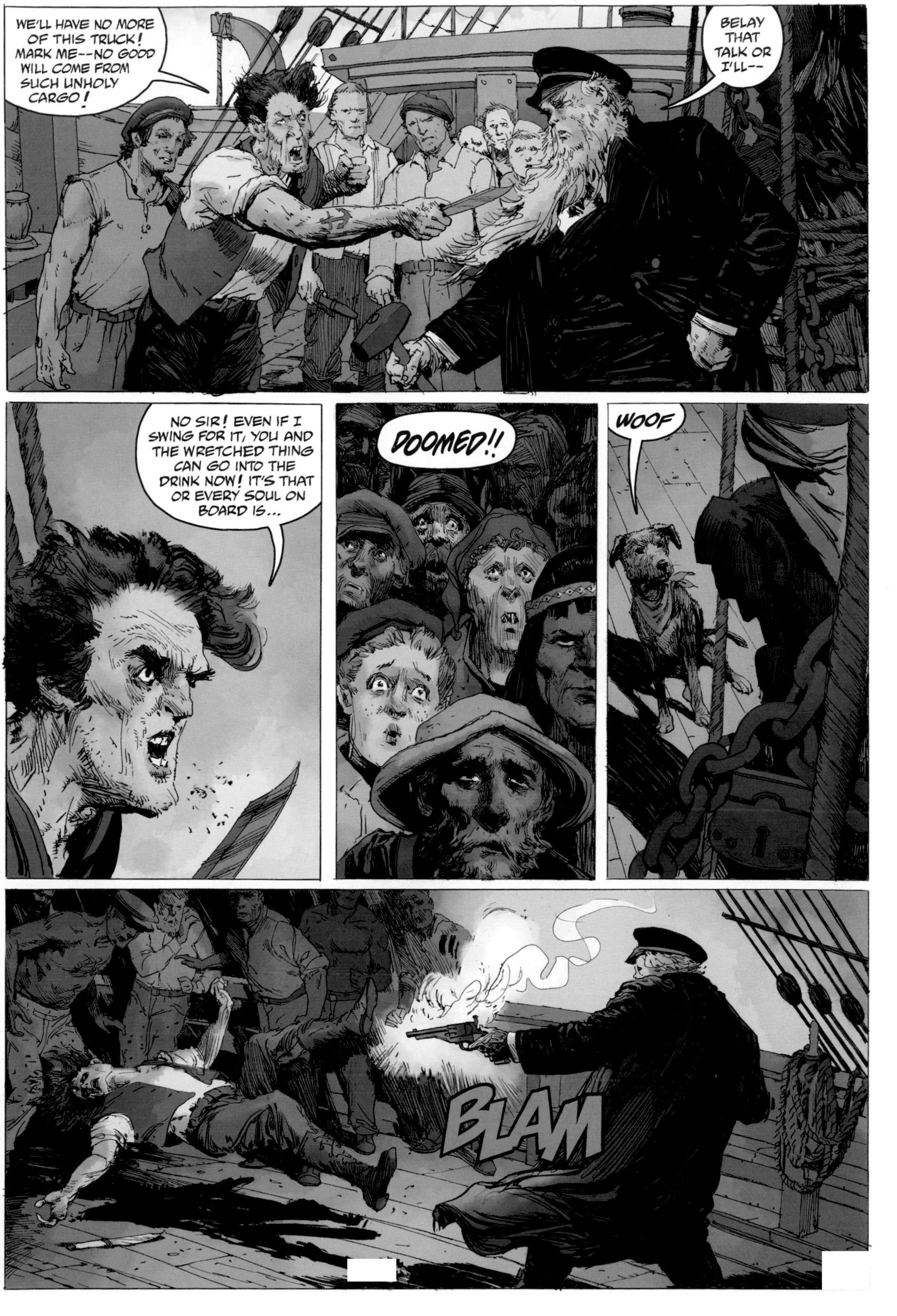
WE'LL HAVE NO MORE OF THIS TRUCK! MARK ME--NO GOOD WILL COME FROM SUCH UNHOLY CARGO!
BELAY THAT TALK OR I'LL--
NO SIR! EVEN IF I SWING FOR IT, YOU AND THE WRETCHED THING CAN GO INTO THE DRINK NOW! IT'S THAT OR EVERY SOUL ON BOARD IS...
DOOMED!!
WOOF
BLAM

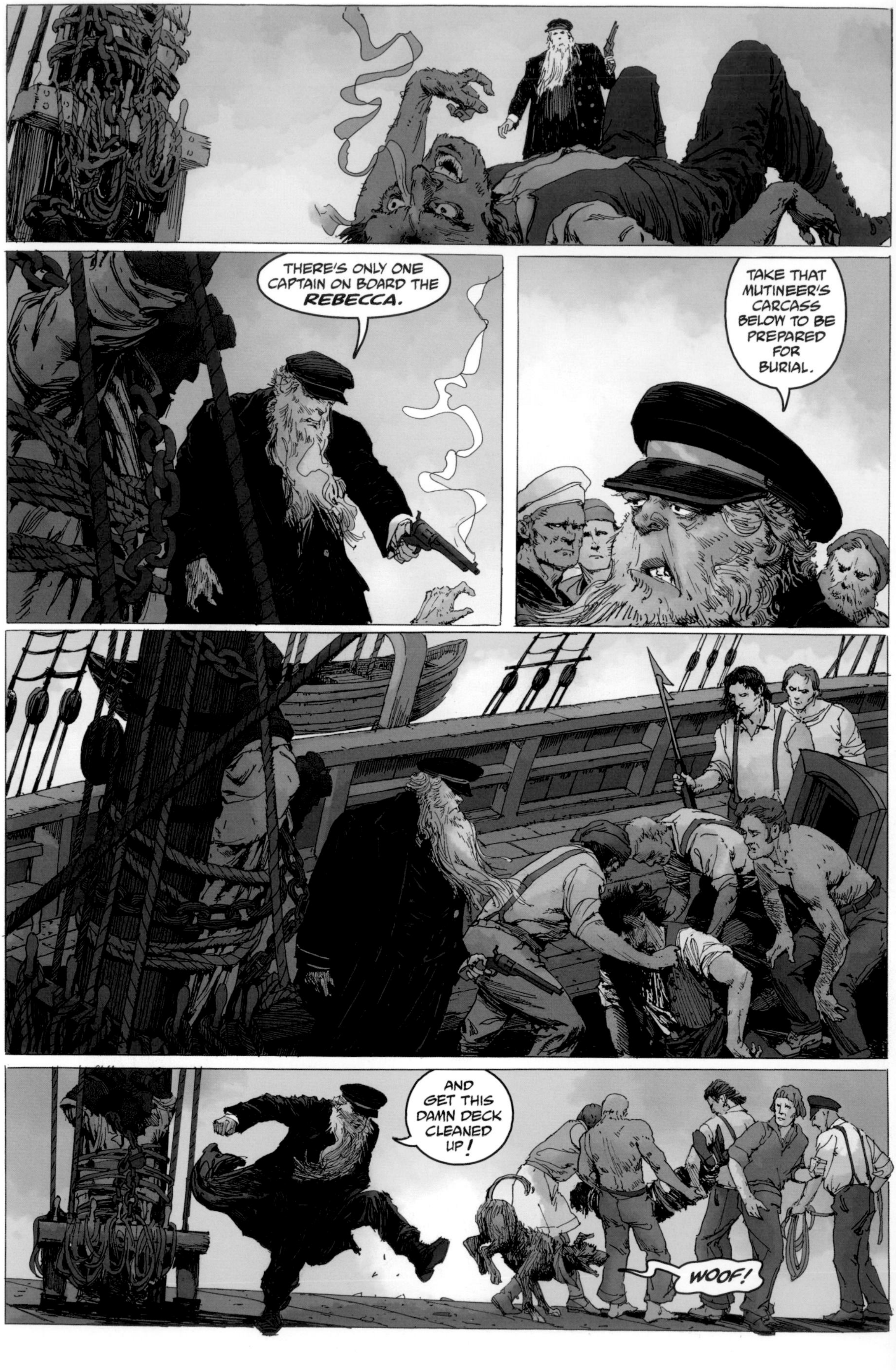
THERE'S ONLY ONE CAPTAIN ON BOARD THE *REBECCA.*
TAKE THAT MUTINEER'S CARCASS BELOW TO BE PREPARED FOR BURIAL.
AND GET THIS DAMN DECK CLEANED UP!
WOOF!

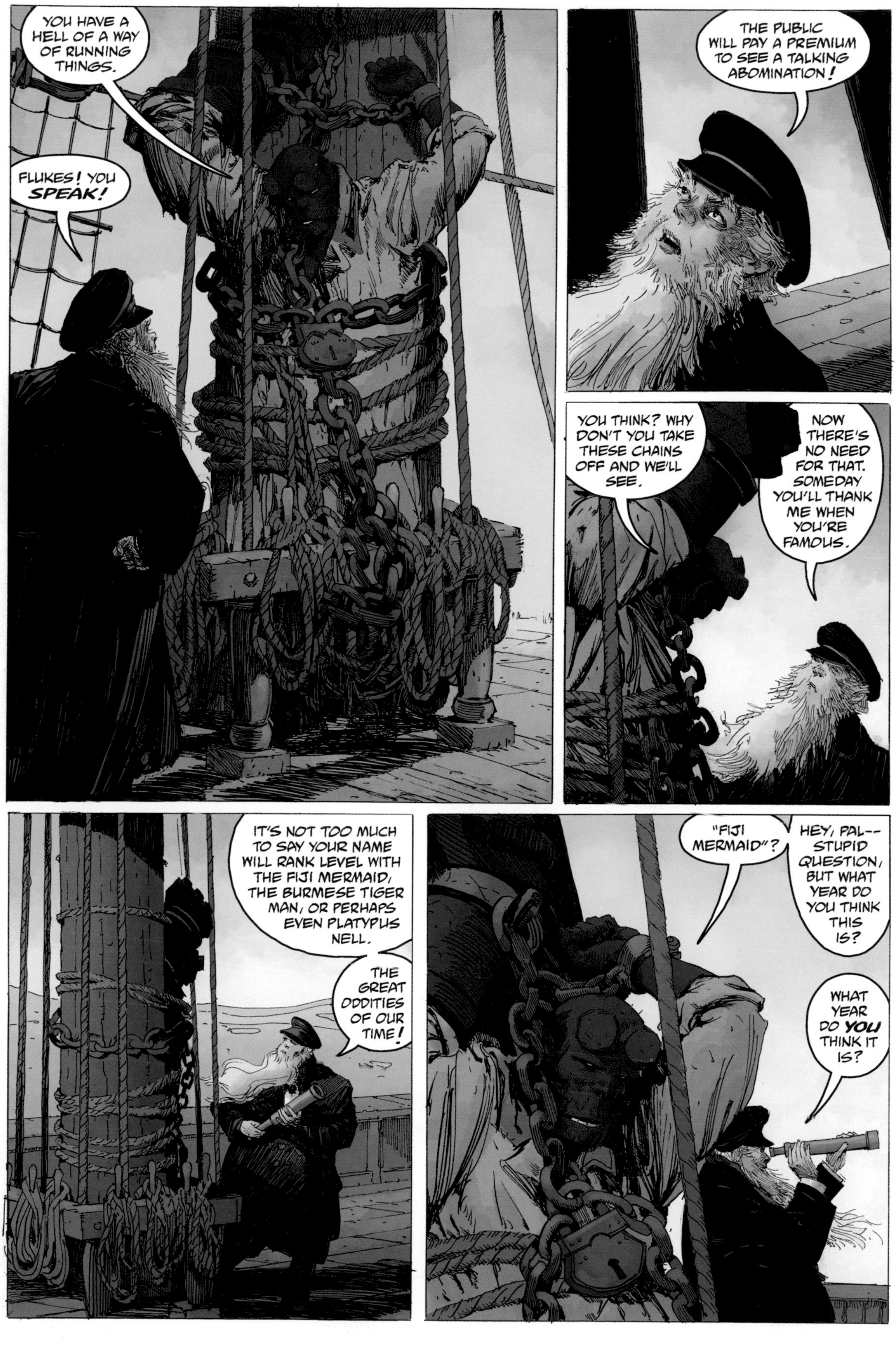
YOU HAVE A HELL OF A WAY OF RUNNING THINGS.
FLUKES! YOU *SPEAK!*
THE PUBLIC WILL PAY A PREMIUM TO SEE A TALKING ABOMINATION!
YOU THINK? WHY DON'T YOU TAKE THESE CHAINS OFF AND WE'LL SEE.
NOW THERE'S NO NEED FOR THAT. SOMEDAY YOU'LL THANK ME WHEN YOU'RE FAMOUS.
IT'S NOT TOO MUCH TO SAY YOUR NAME WILL RANK LEVEL WITH THE FIJI MERMAID, THE BURMESE TIGER MAN, OR PERHAPS EVEN PLATYPUS NELL.
THE GREAT ODDITIES OF OUR TIME!
"FIJI MERMAID"?
HEY, PAL-- STUPID QUESTION, BUT WHAT YEAR DO YOU THINK THIS IS?
WHAT YEAR DO ***YOU*** THINK IT IS?

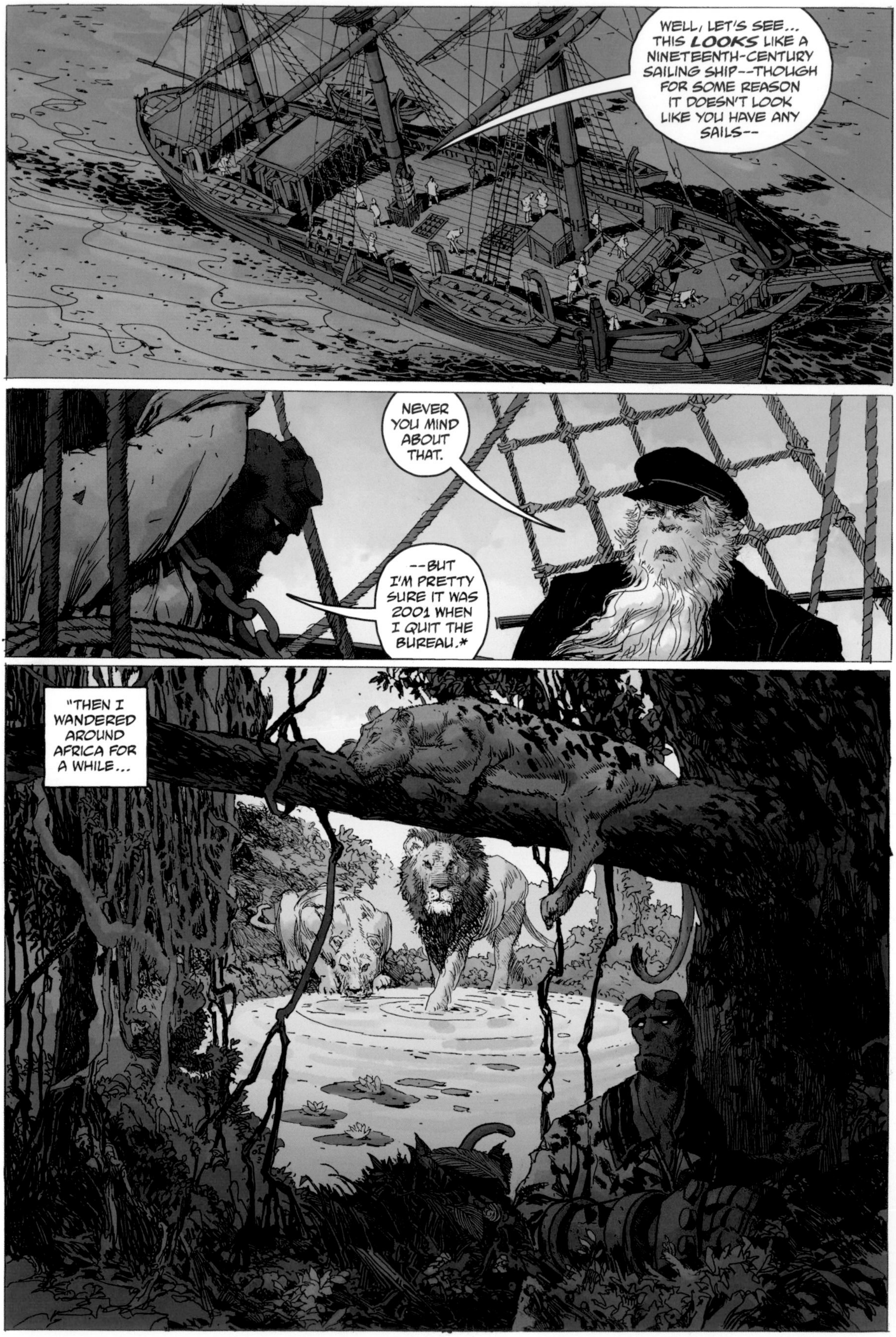
WELL, LET'S SEE... THIS LOOKS LIKE A NINETEENTH-CENTURY SAILING SHIP--THOUGH FOR SOME REASON IT DOESN'T LOOK LIKE YOU HAVE ANY SAILS--
NEVER YOU MIND ABOUT THAT.
--BUT I'M PRETTY SURE IT WAS 2001 WHEN I QUIT THE BUREAU.*
"THEN I WANDERED AROUND AFRICA FOR A WHILE...

*SEE **HELLBOY: CONQUEROR WORM**

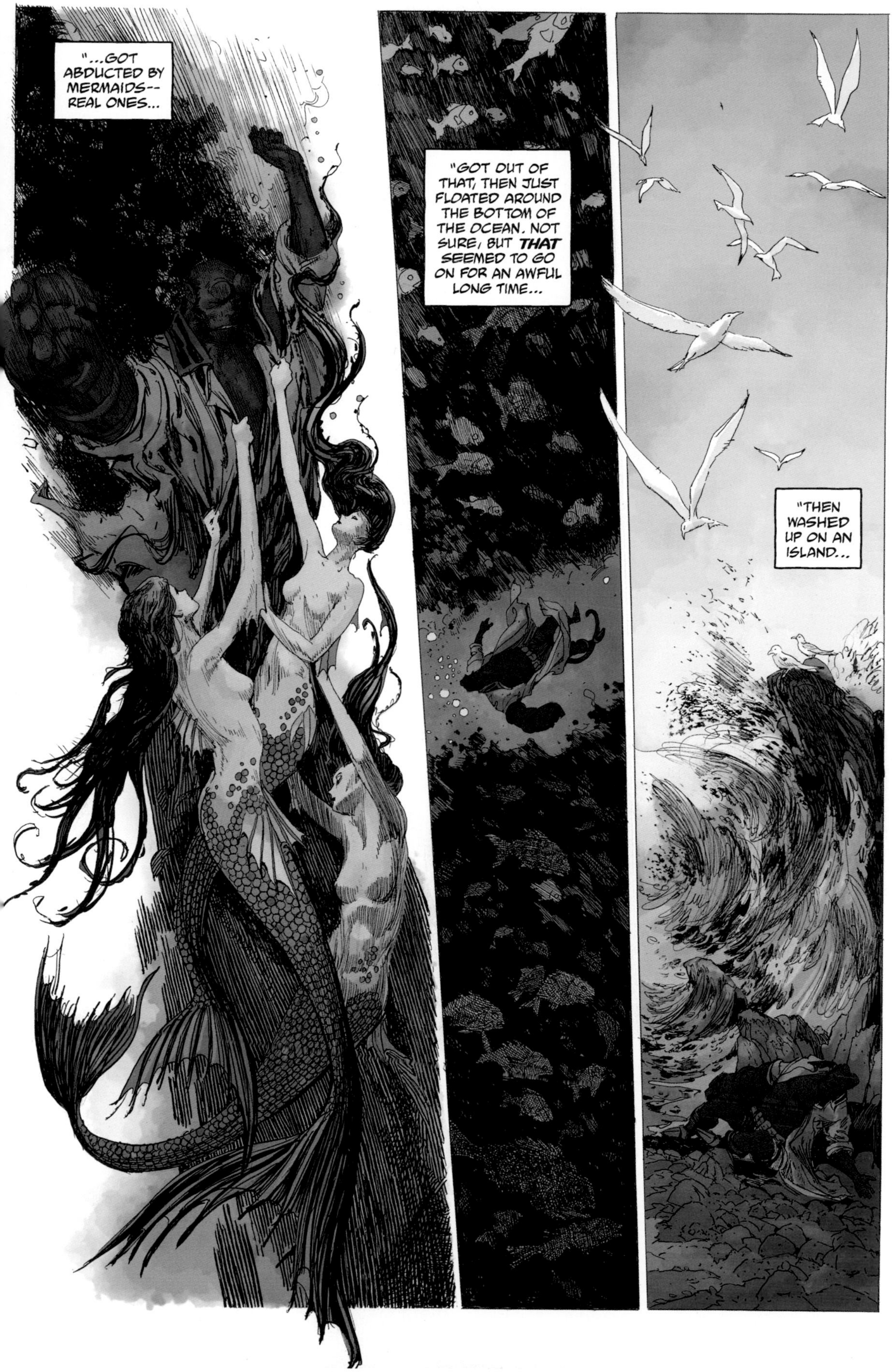
"...GOT ABDUCTED BY MERMAIDS--REAL ONES...
"GOT OUT OF THAT, THEN JUST FLOATED AROUND THE BOTTOM OF THE OCEAN. NOT SURE, BUT THAT SEEMED TO GO ON FOR AN AWFUL LONG TIME...
"THEN WASHED UP ON AN ISLAND...

"...WHERE A WHOLE LOT OF OTHER HORRIBLE STUFF HAPPENED."*

LET THE PEOPLE COME UNTO ME, AND AT LEAST SOME OF THEM WILL LIVE.

HERE WE GO.

AFTER THAT THINGS DO GET A LITTLE BLURRY. THERE WAS A BOAT--

GAD, YOU SPOUT SOME COLORFUL YARNS. P.T. BARNUM NEVER HAD SUCH A CURIOSITY! A CRAZED MONSTER!

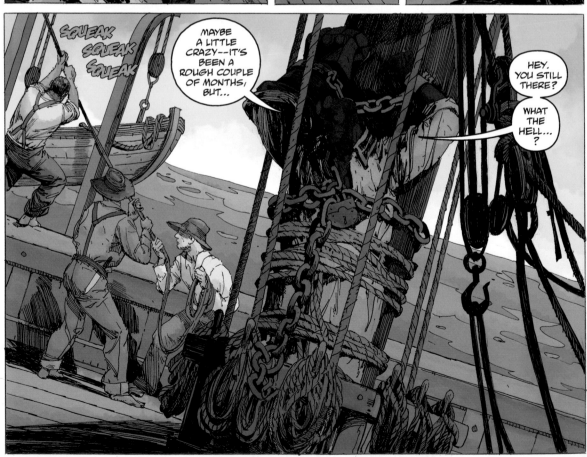

SQUEAK SQUEAK SQUEAK

MAYBE A LITTLE CRAZY--IT'S BEEN A ROUGH COUPLE OF MONTHS, BUT...

HEY, YOU STILL THERE?

WHAT THE HELL...?

*THIS STORY TAKES PLACE FOLLOWING THE EVENTS IN *HELLBOY: STRANGE PLACES*

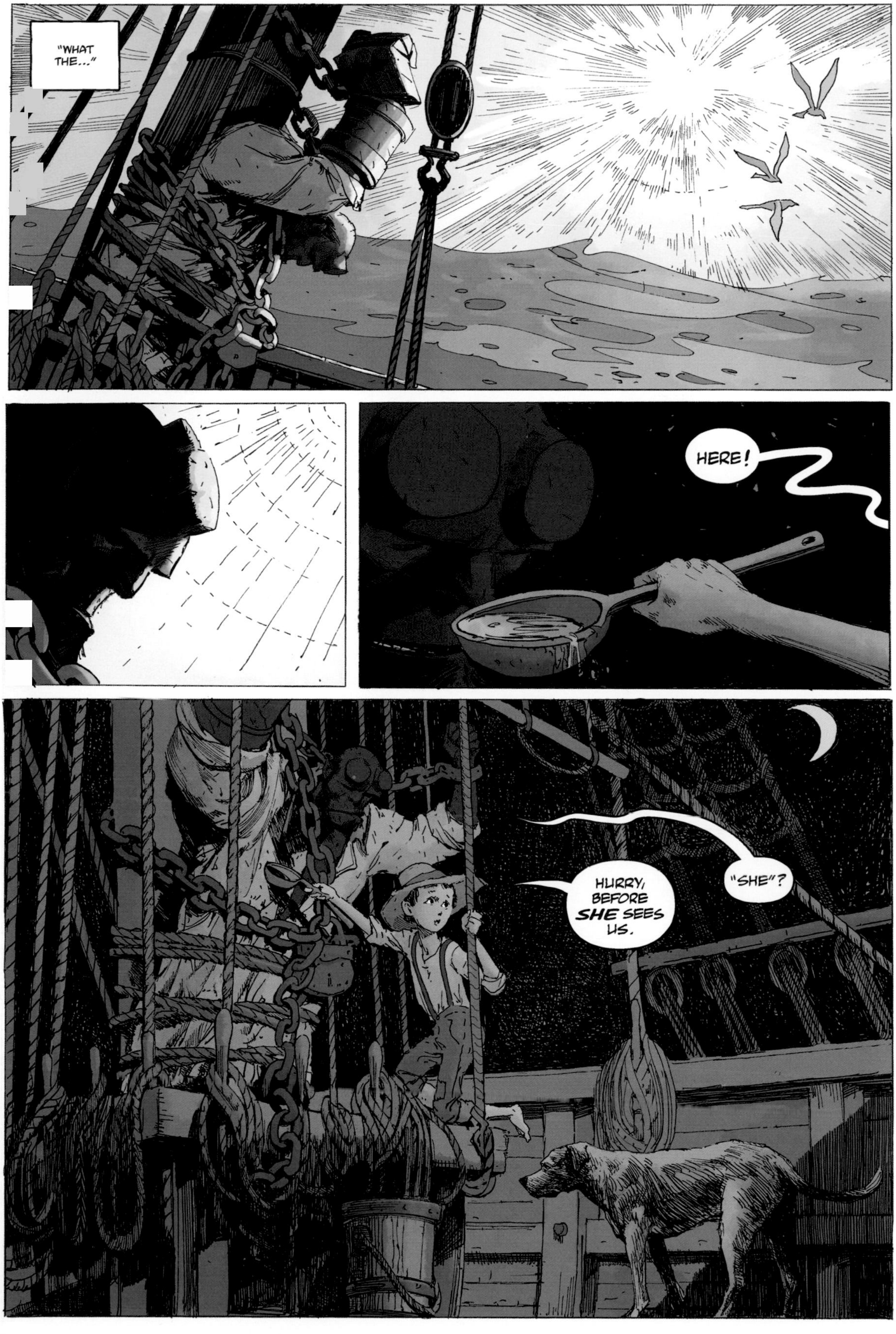
"WHAT THE..."
HERE!
HURRY, BEFORE SHE SEES US.
"SHE"?

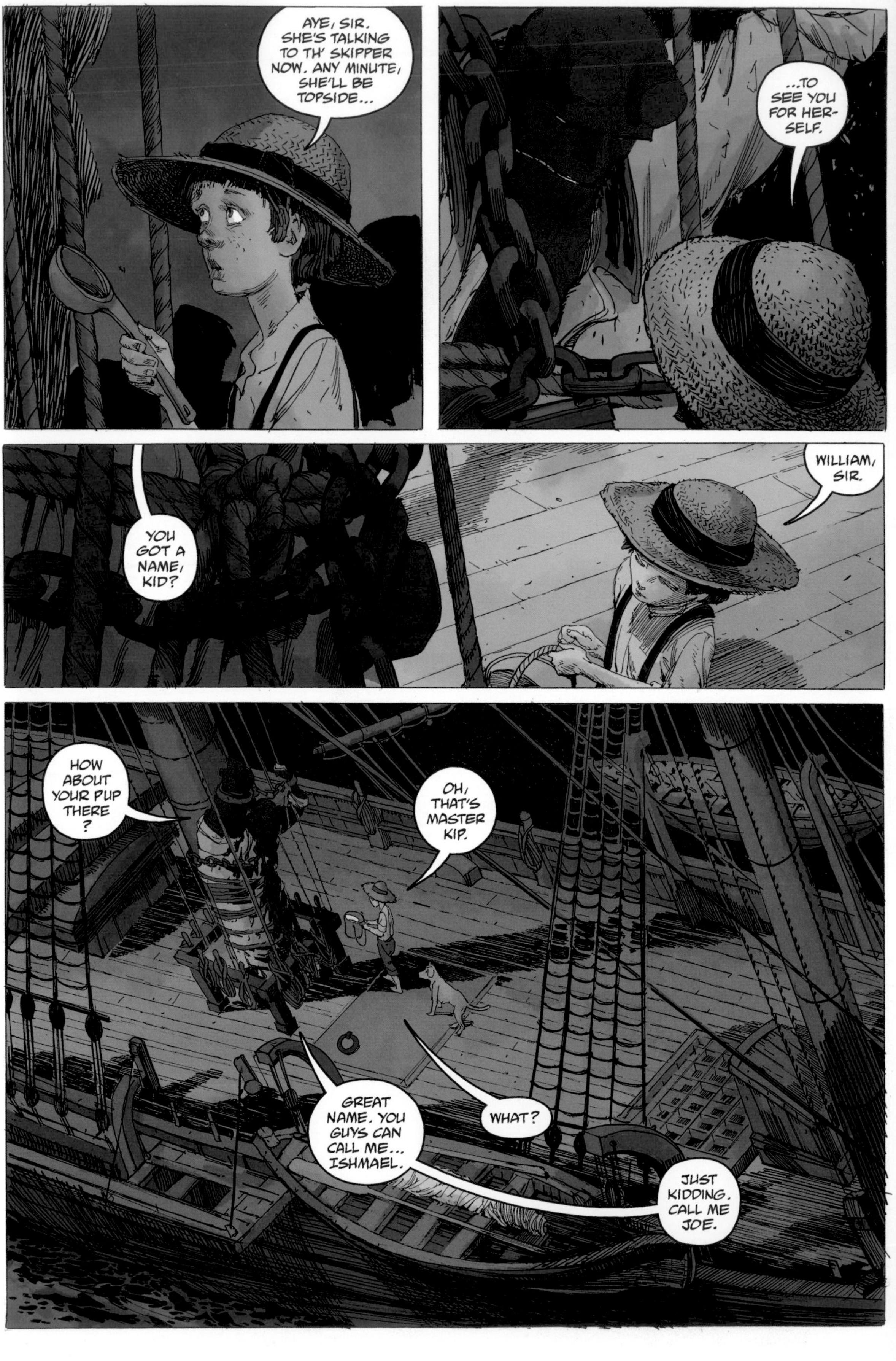
AYE, SIR. SHE'S TALKING TO TH' SKIPPER NOW. ANY MINUTE, SHE'LL BE TOPSIDE...
...TO SEE YOU FOR HER-SELF.
YOU GOT A NAME, KID?
WILLIAM, SIR.
HOW ABOUT YOUR PUP THERE ?
OH, THAT'S MASTER KIP.
GREAT NAME. YOU GUYS CAN CALL ME... ISHMAEL.
WHAT?
JUST KIDDING. CALL ME JOE.

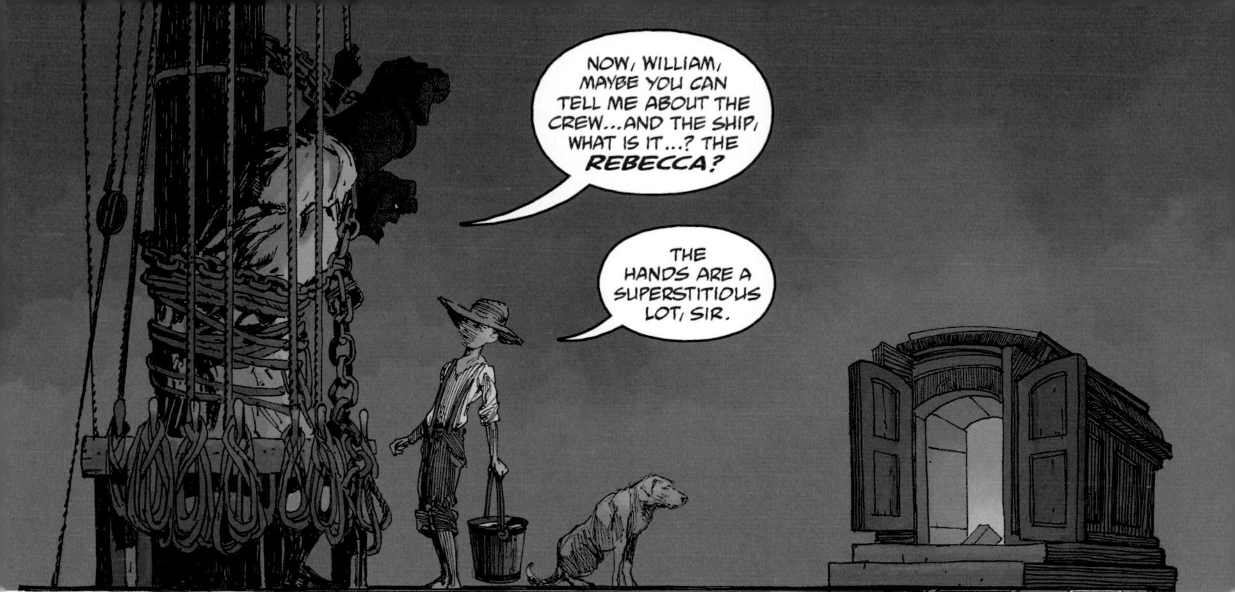
NOW, WILLIAM, MAYBE YOU CAN TELL ME ABOUT THE CREW...AND THE SHIP, WHAT IS IT...? THE *REBECCA?*
THE HANDS ARE A SUPERSTITIOUS LOT, SIR.

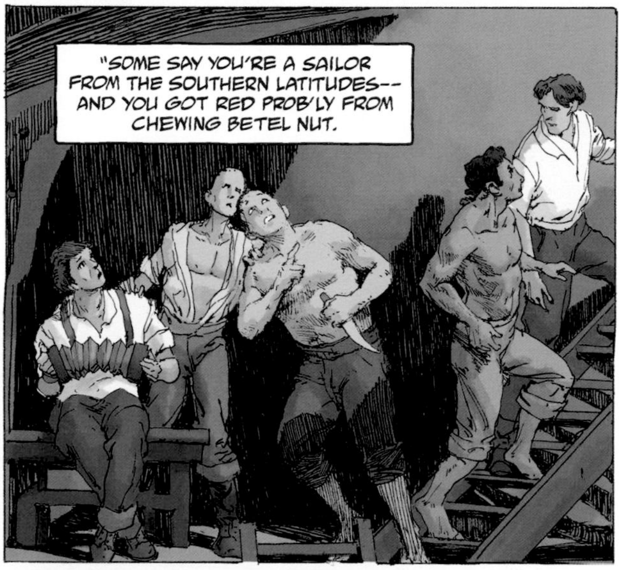
"SOME SAY YOU'RE A SAILOR FROM THE SOUTHERN LATITUDES-- AND YOU GOT RED PROB'LY FROM CHEWING BETEL NUT.

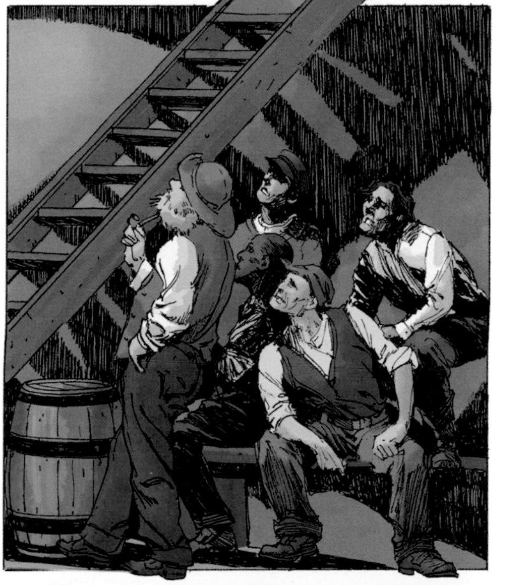

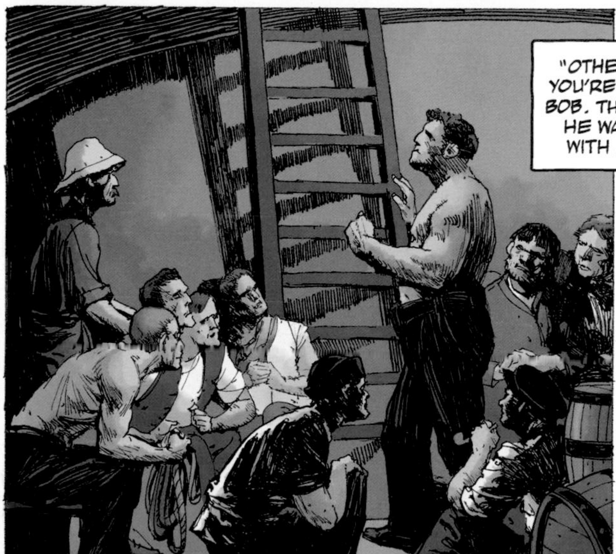
"OTHERS THINK YOU'RE PIG-IRON BOB. THEY HEARD HE WAS BORN WITH A TAIL...

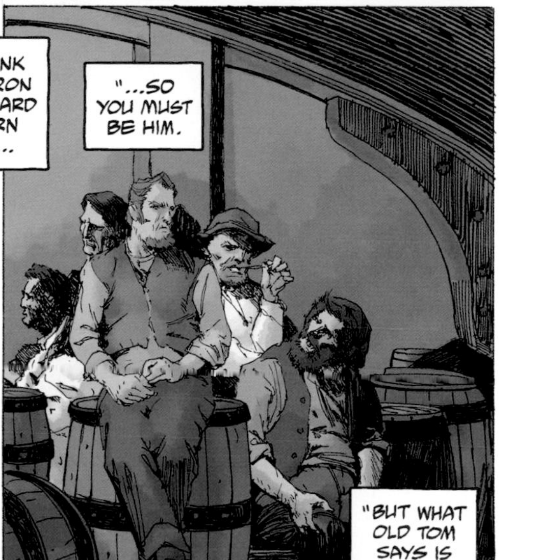
"...SO YOU MUST BE HIM.
"BUT WHAT OLD TOM SAYS IS DEAD SET AGAINST YOU..."

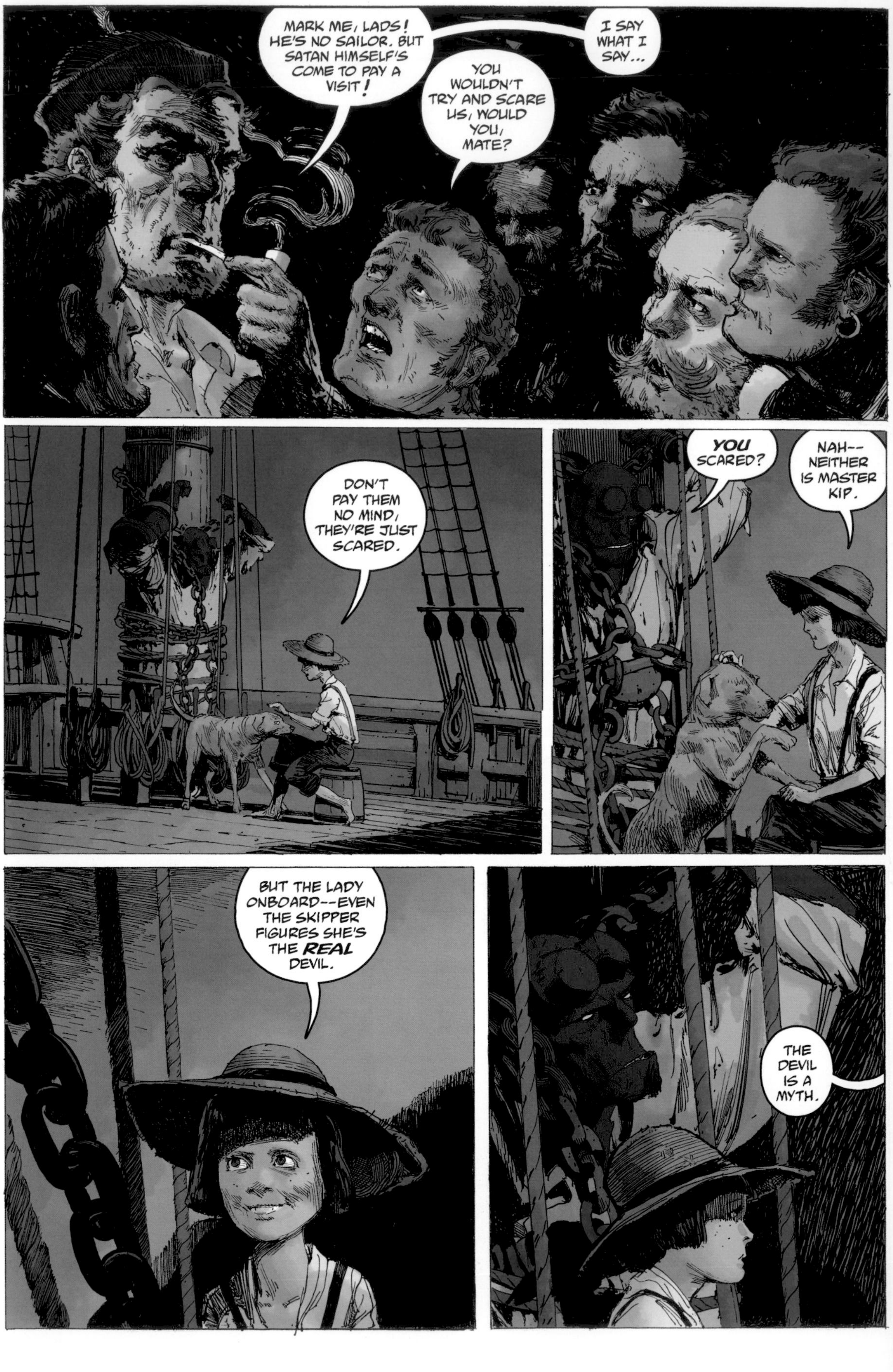
MARK ME, LADS! HE'S NO SAILOR. BUT SATAN HIMSELF'S COME TO PAY A VISIT!
I SAY WHAT I SAY...
YOU WOULDN'T TRY AND SCARE US, WOULD YOU, MATE?
DON'T PAY THEM NO MIND, THEY'RE JUST SCARED.
YOU SCARED?
NAH-- NEITHER IS MASTER KIP.
BUT THE LADY ONBOARD--EVEN THE SKIPPER FIGURES SHE'S THE REAL DEVIL.
THE DEVIL IS A MYTH.

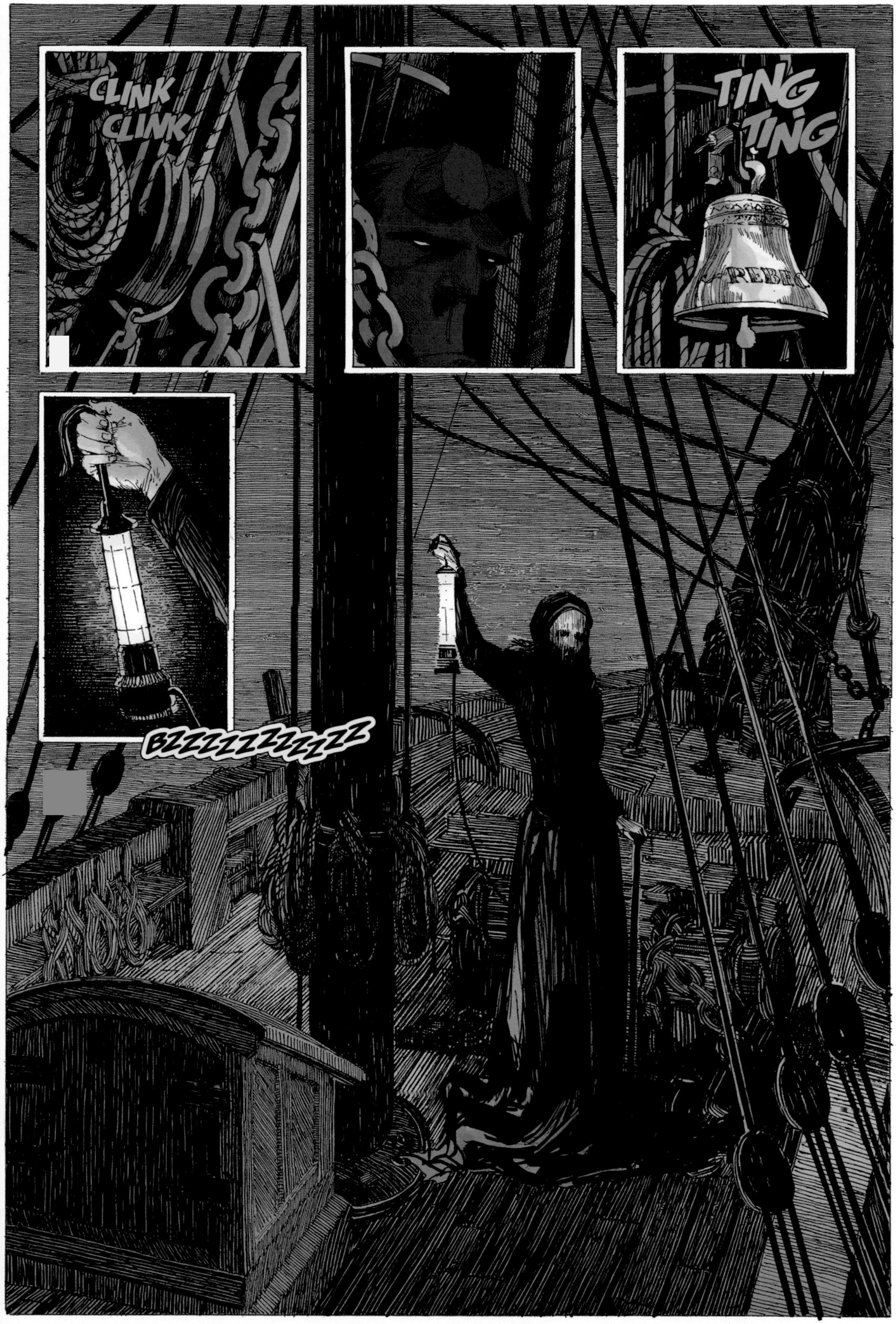
CLINK
CLINK
TING
TING
BZZZZZZZZZZZ

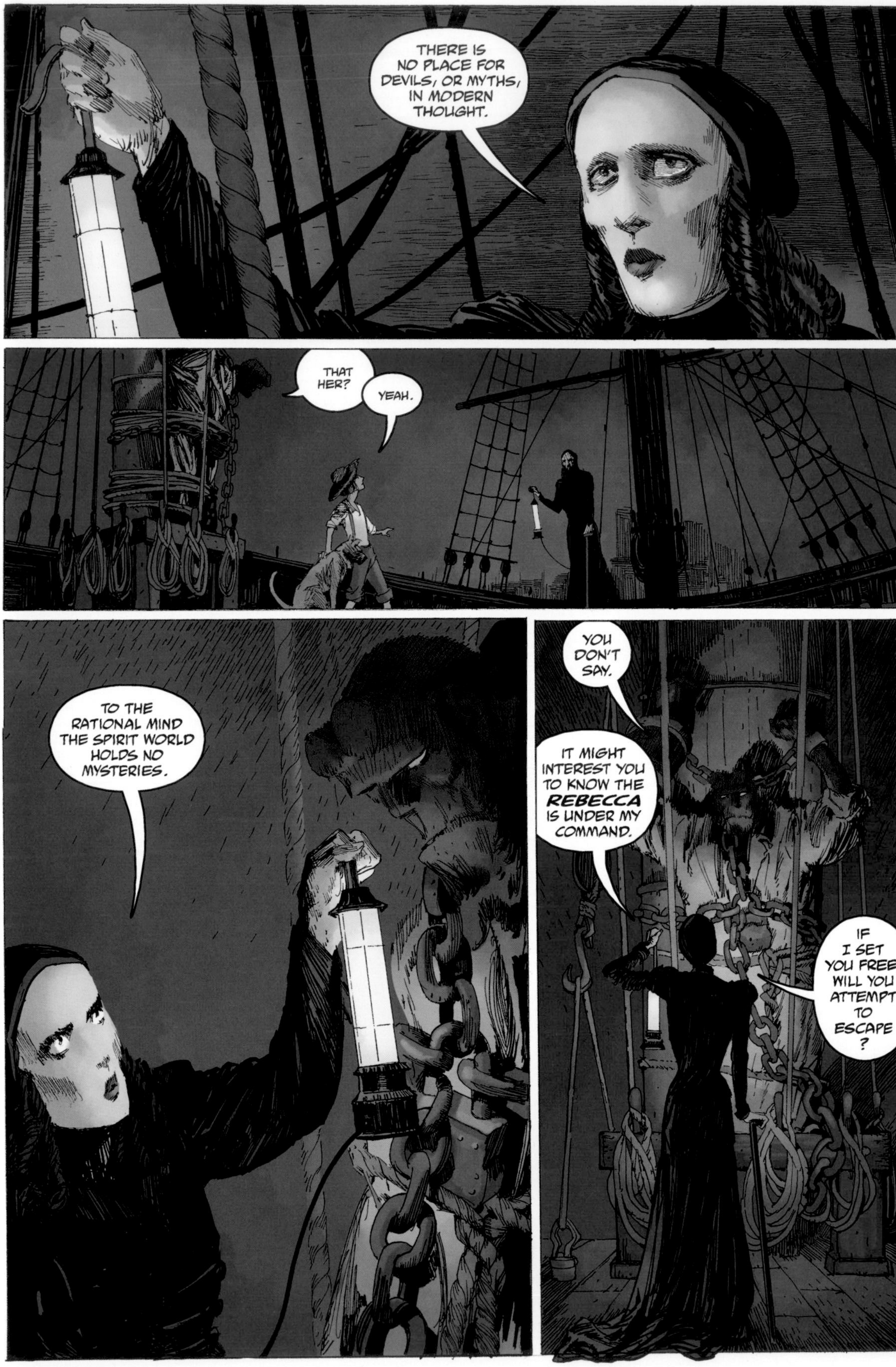
THERE IS NO PLACE FOR DEVILS, OR MYTHS, IN MODERN THOUGHT.
THAT HER?
YEAH.
TO THE RATIONAL MIND THE SPIRIT WORLD HOLDS NO MYSTERIES.
YOU DON'T SAY.
IT MIGHT INTEREST YOU TO KNOW THE REBECCA IS UNDER MY COMMAND.
IF I SET YOU FREE, WILL YOU ATTEMPT TO ESCAPE ?

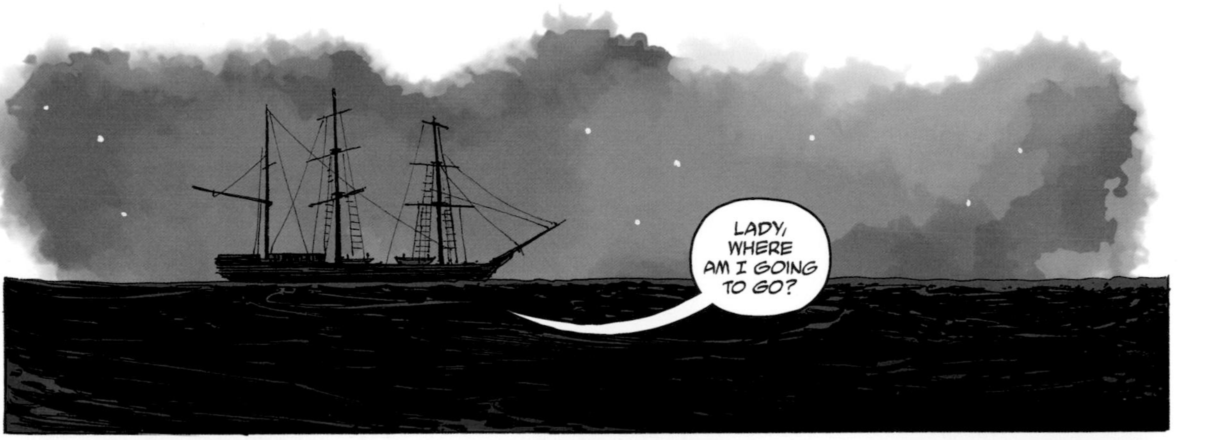
LADY, WHERE AM I GOING TO GO?

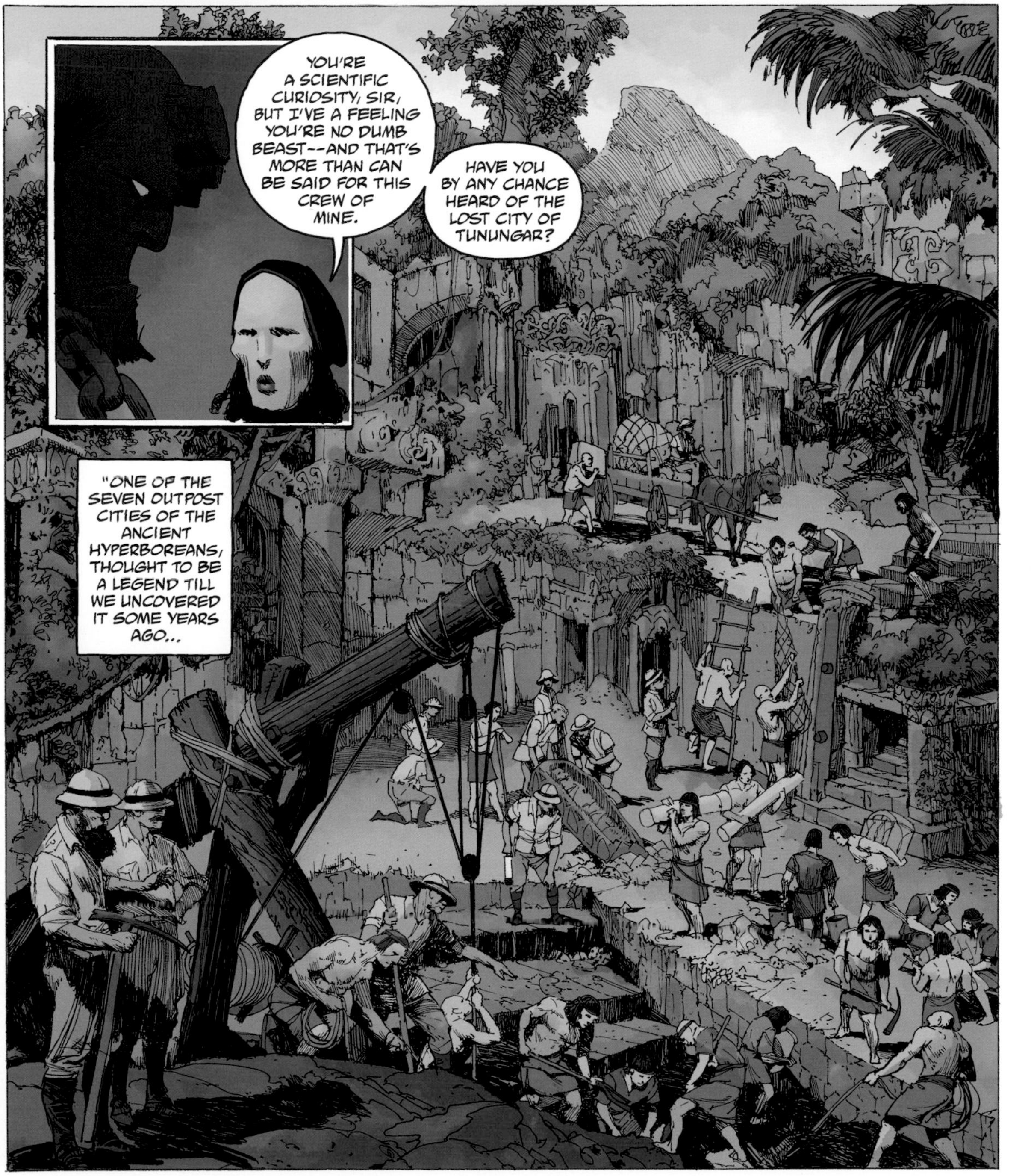
YOU'RE A SCIENTIFIC CURIOSITY, SIR, BUT I'VE A FEELING YOU'RE NO DUMB BEAST--AND THAT'S MORE THAN CAN BE SAID FOR THIS CREW OF MINE.
HAVE YOU BY ANY CHANCE HEARD OF THE LOST CITY OF TUNUNGAR?
"ONE OF THE SEVEN OUTPOST CITIES OF THE ANCIENT HYPERBOREANS, THOUGHT TO BE A LEGEND TILL WE UNCOVERED IT SOME YEARS AGO...

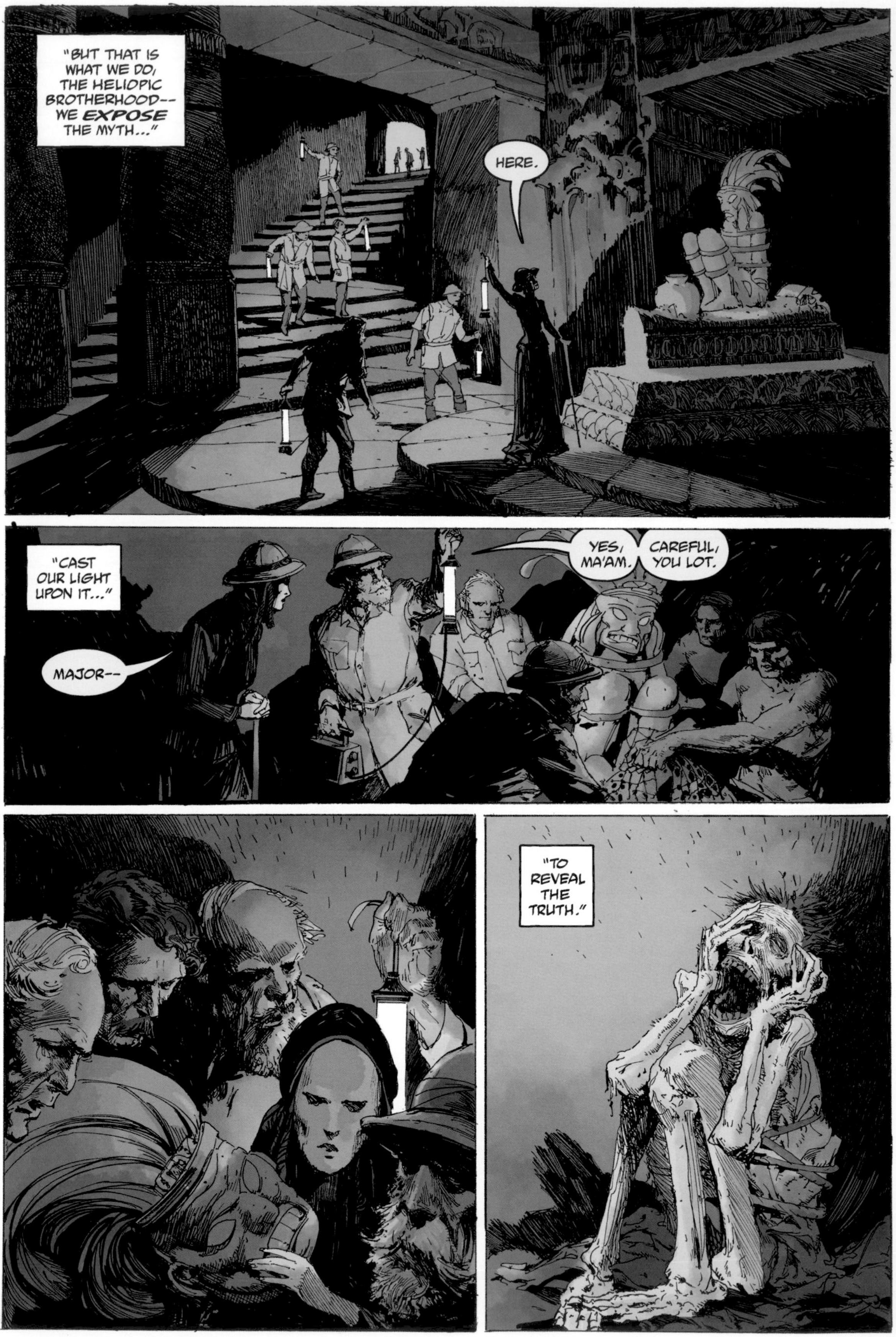
"BUT THAT IS WHAT WE DO, THE HELIOPIC BROTHERHOOD-- WE EXPOSE THE MYTH..."
HERE.
"CAST OUR LIGHT UPON IT..."
MAJOR--
YES, MA'AM.
CAREFUL, YOU LOT.
"TO REVEAL THE TRUTH."

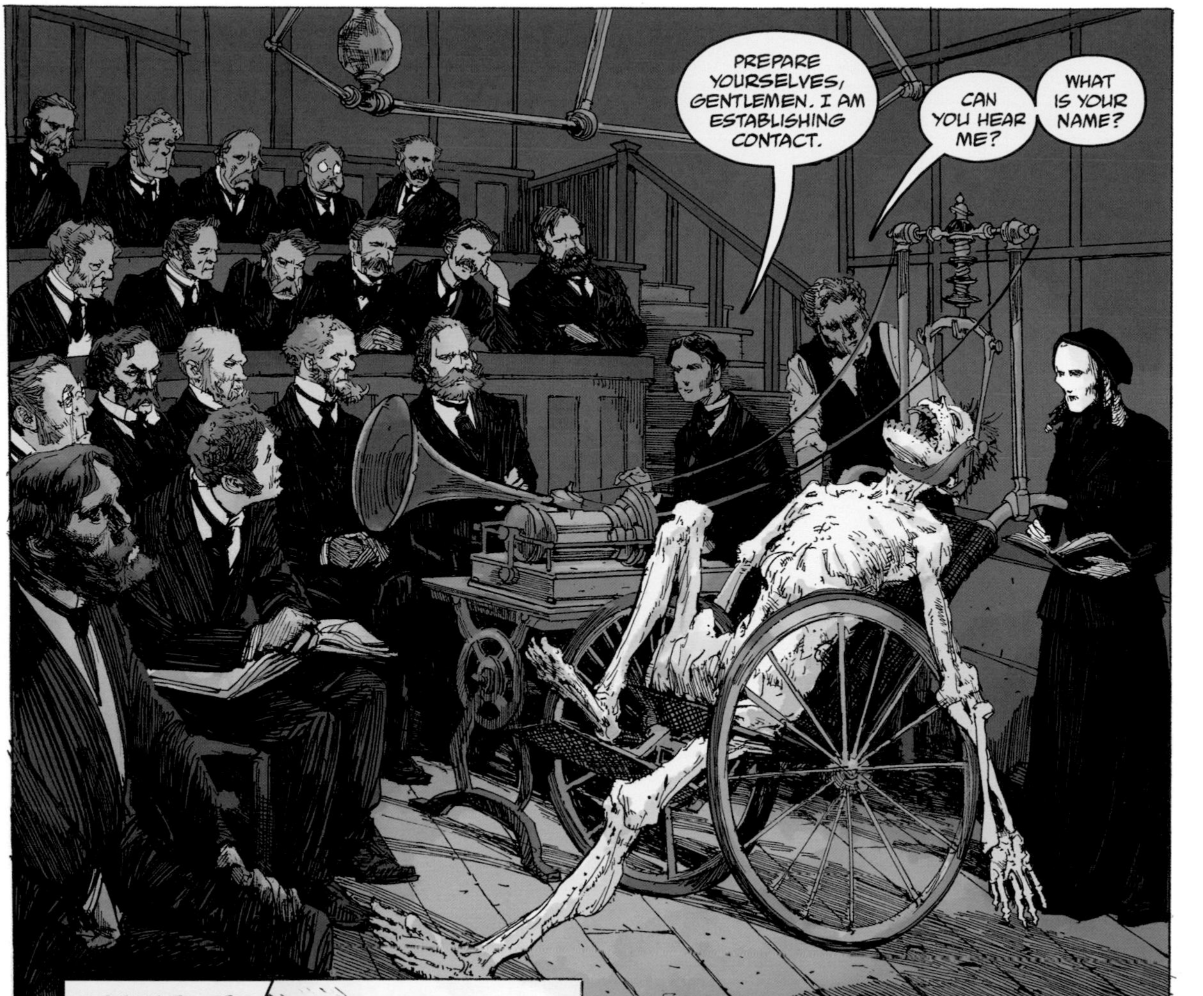
PREPARE YOURSELVES, GENTLEMEN. I AM ESTABLISHING CONTACT.
CAN YOU HEAR ME?
WHAT IS YOUR NAME?

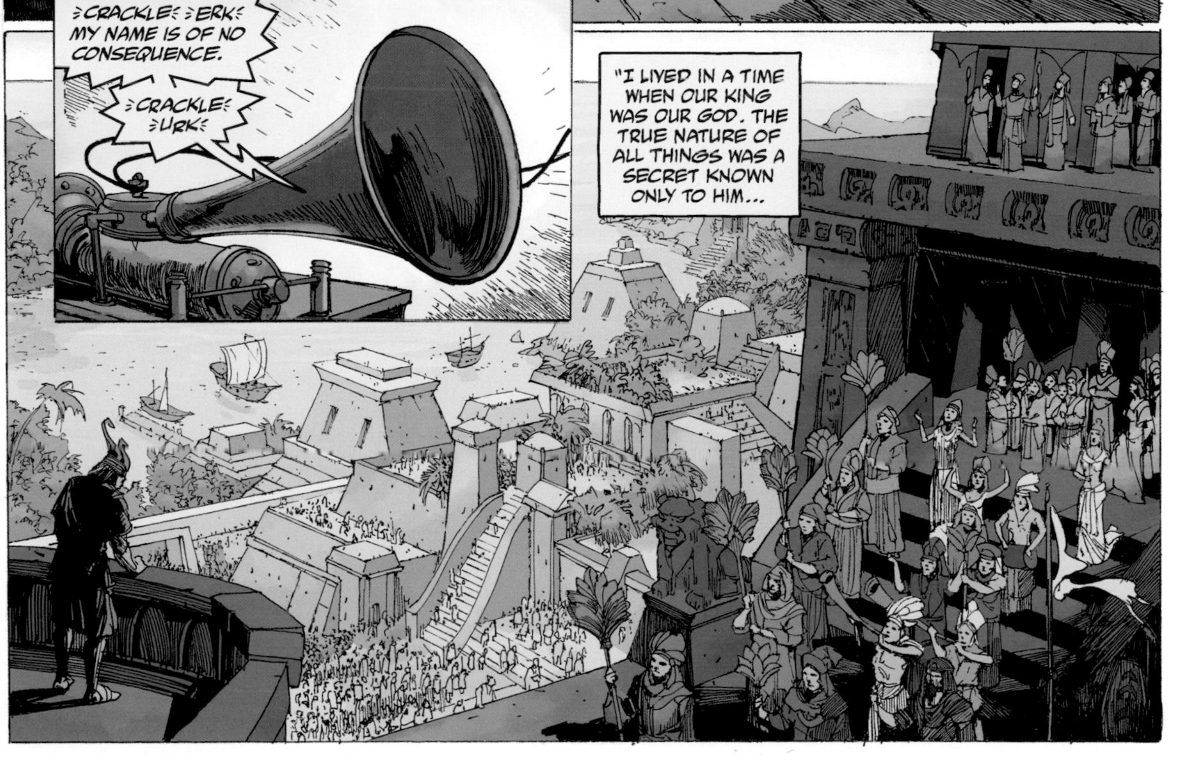
CRACKLE ERK MY NAME IS OF NO CONSEQUENCE.
CRACKLE URK
"I LIVED IN A TIME WHEN OUR KING WAS OUR GOD. THE TRUE NATURE OF ALL THINGS WAS A SECRET KNOWN ONLY TO HIM...

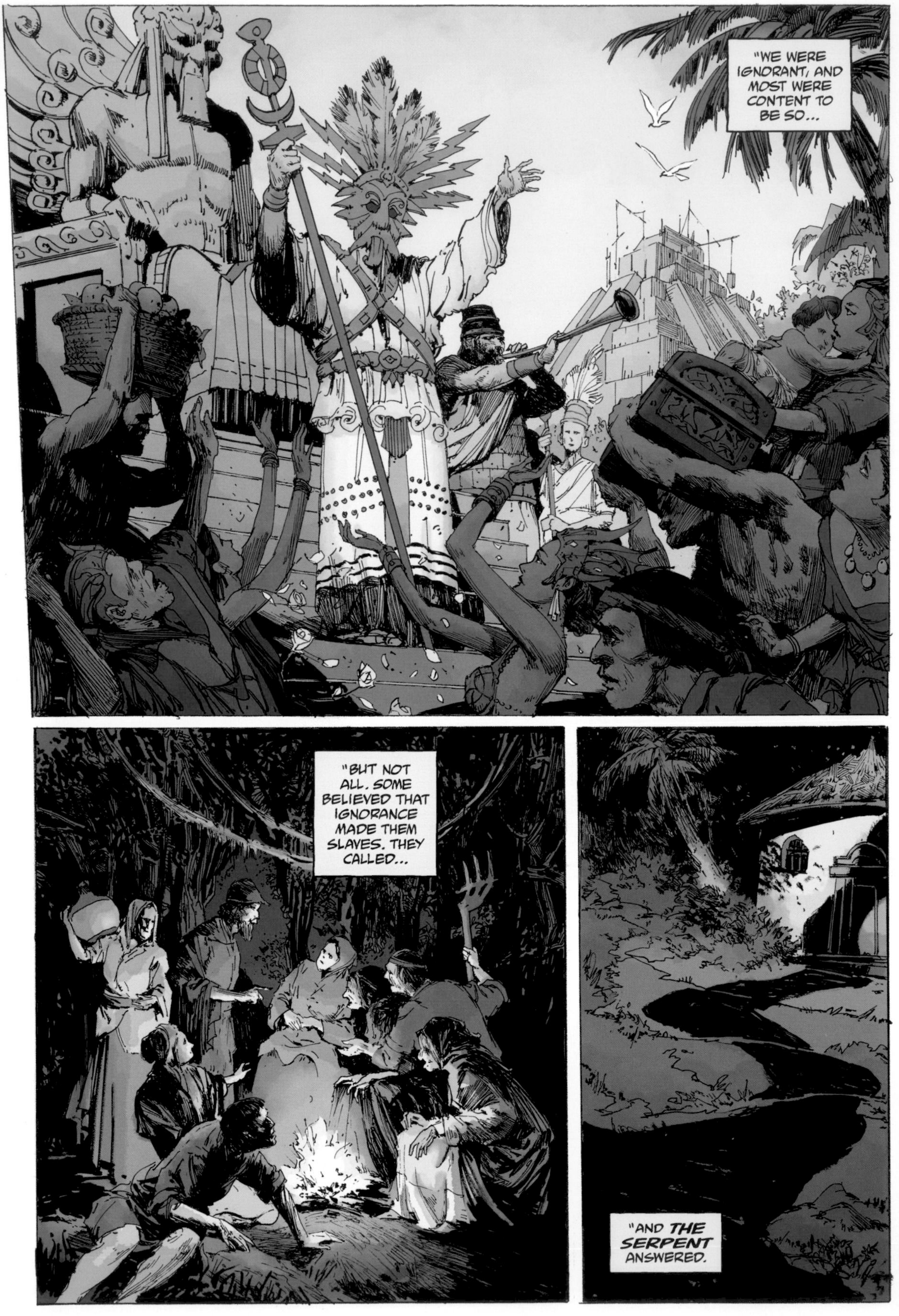
"WE WERE IGNORANT, AND MOST WERE CONTENT TO BE SO...
"BUT NOT ALL. SOME BELIEVED THAT IGNORANCE MADE THEM SLAVES. THEY CALLED...
"AND THE SERPENT ANSWERED.

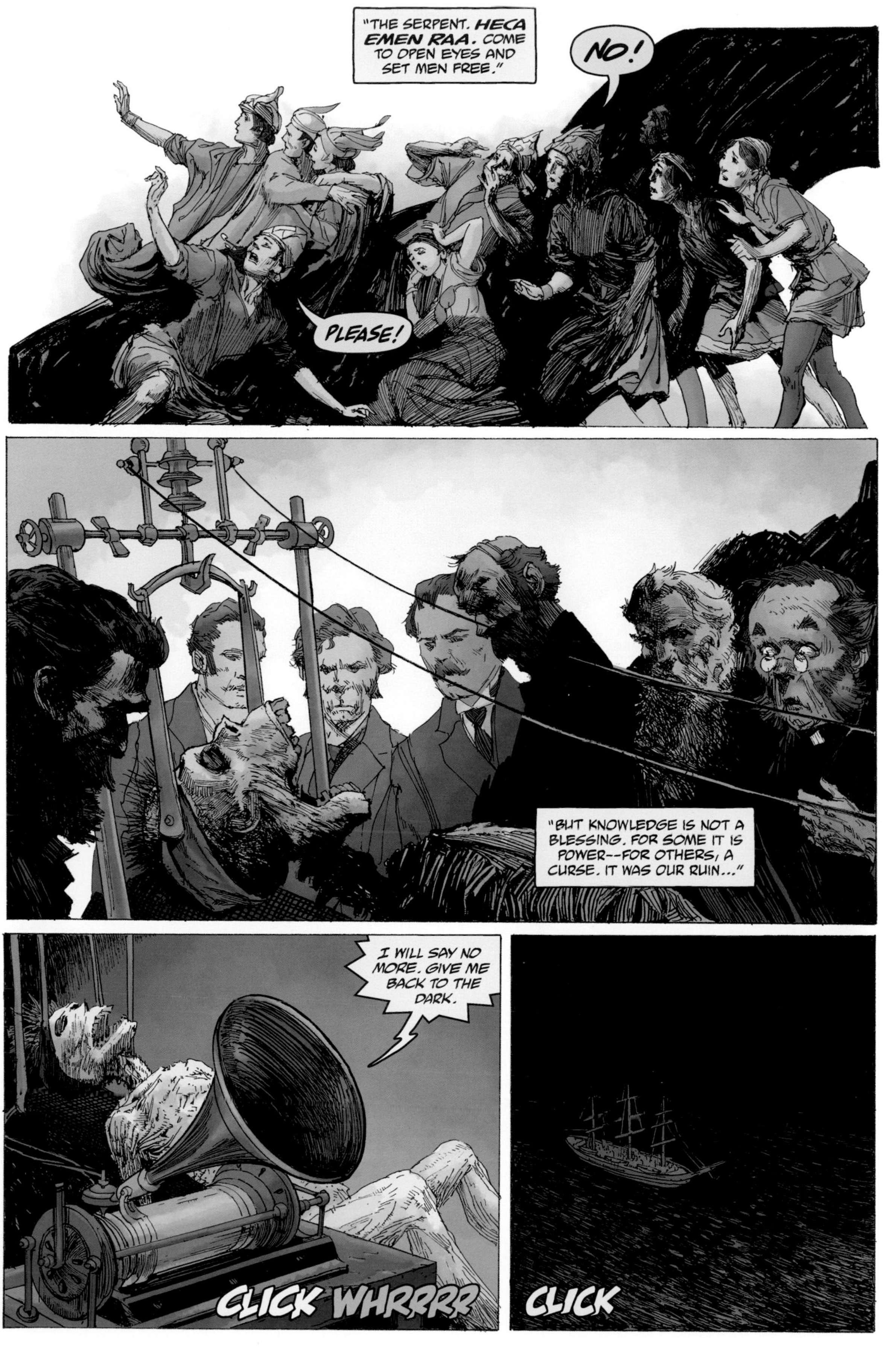
"THE SERPENT. HECA EMEN RAA. COME TO OPEN EYES AND SET MEN FREE."
NO!
PLEASE!
"BUT KNOWLEDGE IS NOT A BLESSING. FOR SOME IT IS POWER--FOR OTHERS, A CURSE. IT WAS OUR RUIN..."
I WILL SAY NO MORE. GIVE ME BACK TO THE DARK.
CLICK WHRRRR
CLICK

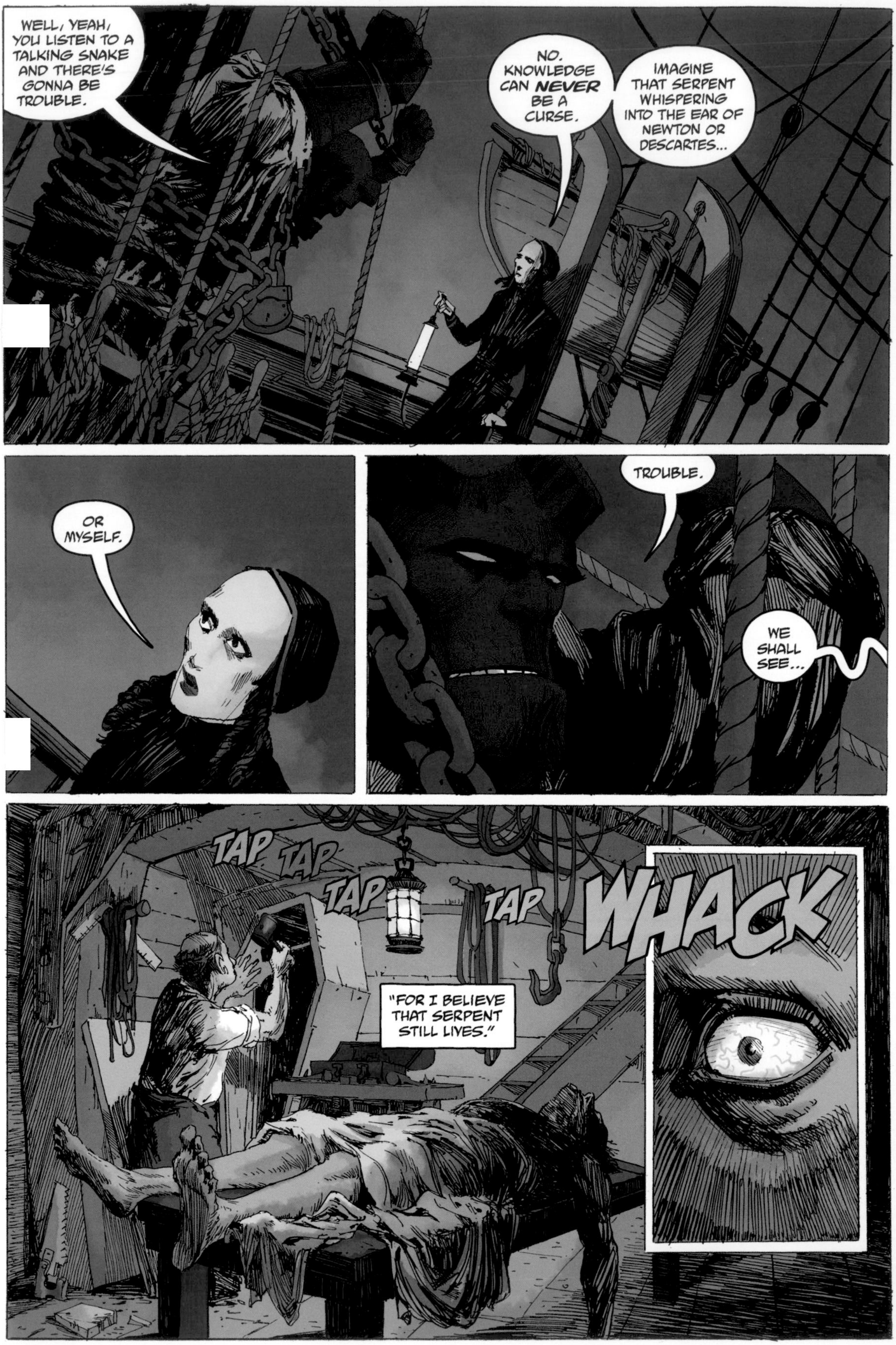
WELL, YEAH, YOU LISTEN TO A TALKING SNAKE AND THERE'S GONNA BE TROUBLE.
NO. KNOWLEDGE CAN NEVER BE A CURSE.
IMAGINE THAT SERPENT WHISPERING INTO THE EAR OF NEWTON OR DESCARTES...
OR MYSELF.
TROUBLE.
WE SHALL SEE...
TAP TAP
TAP
TAP
WHACK
"FOR I BELIEVE THAT SERPENT STILL LIVES."

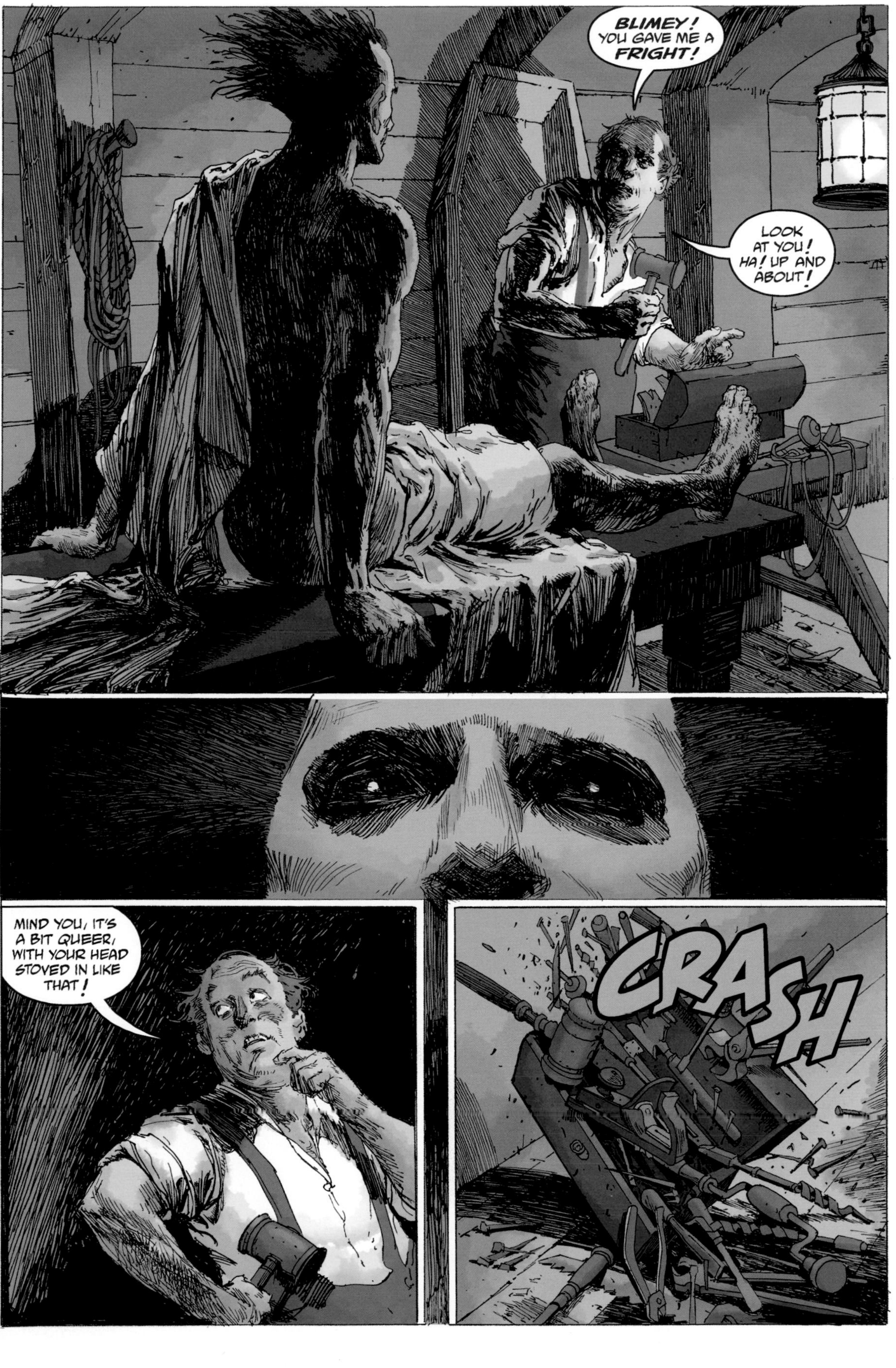
BLIMEY! YOU GAVE ME A FRIGHT!
LOOK AT YOU! HA! UP AND ABOUT!
MIND YOU, IT'S A BIT QUEER, WITH YOUR HEAD STOVED IN LIKE THAT!
CRASH

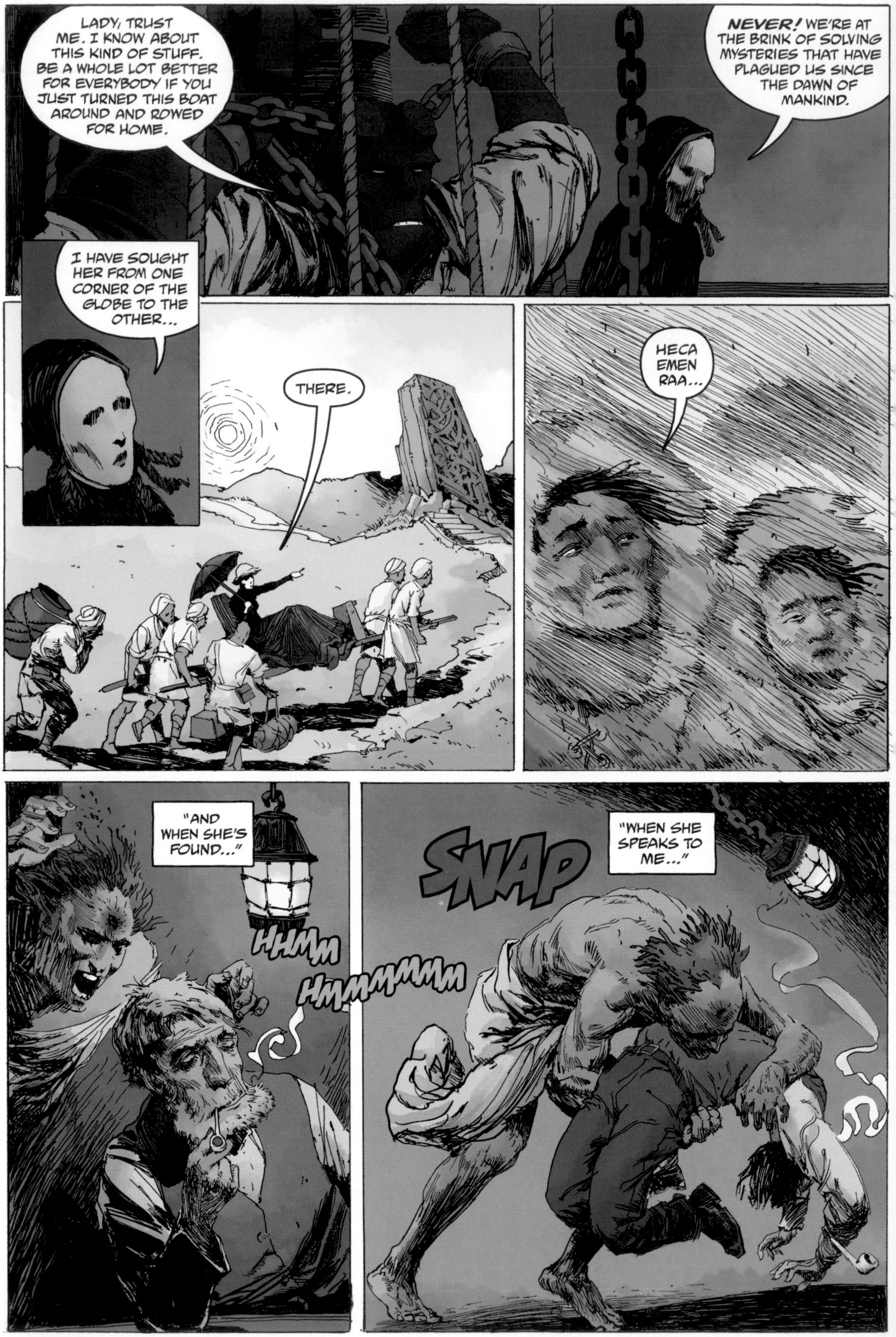

LADY, TRUST ME. I KNOW ABOUT THIS KIND OF STUFF. BE A WHOLE LOT BETTER FOR EVERYBODY IF YOU JUST TURNED THIS BOAT AROUND AND ROWED FOR HOME.
NEVER! WE'RE AT THE BRINK OF SOLVING MYSTERIES THAT HAVE PLAGUED US SINCE THE DAWN OF MANKIND.
I HAVE SOUGHT HER FROM ONE CORNER OF THE GLOBE TO THE OTHER...
THERE.
HECA EMEN RAA...
"AND WHEN SHE'S FOUND..."
HHMM
HMMMMMM
SNAP
"WHEN SHE SPEAKS TO ME..."

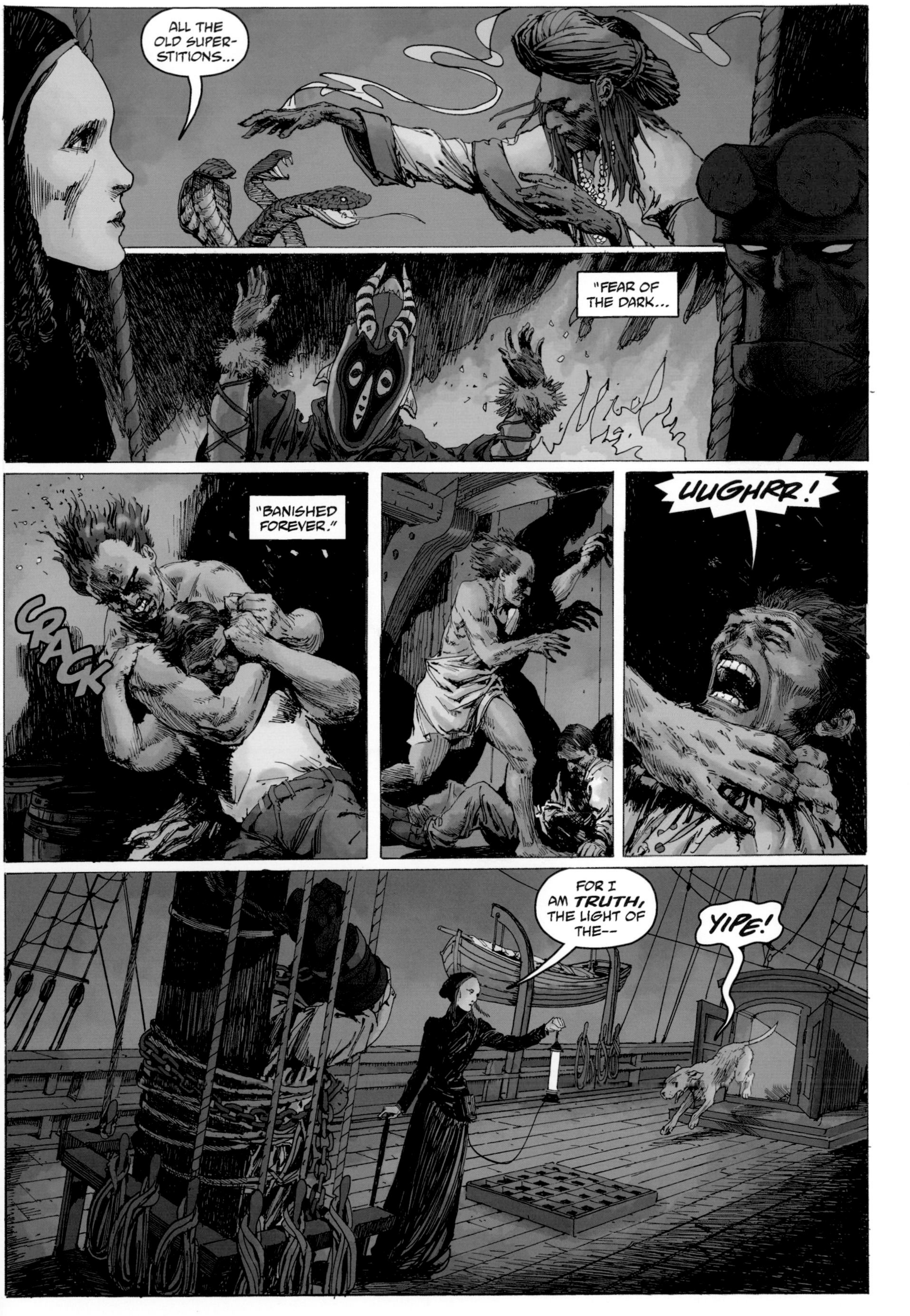
ALL THE OLD SUPER-STITIONS...
"FEAR OF THE DARK...
"BANISHED FOREVER."
CRACK
UUGHRR!
FOR I AM TRUTH, THE LIGHT OF THE--
YIPE!

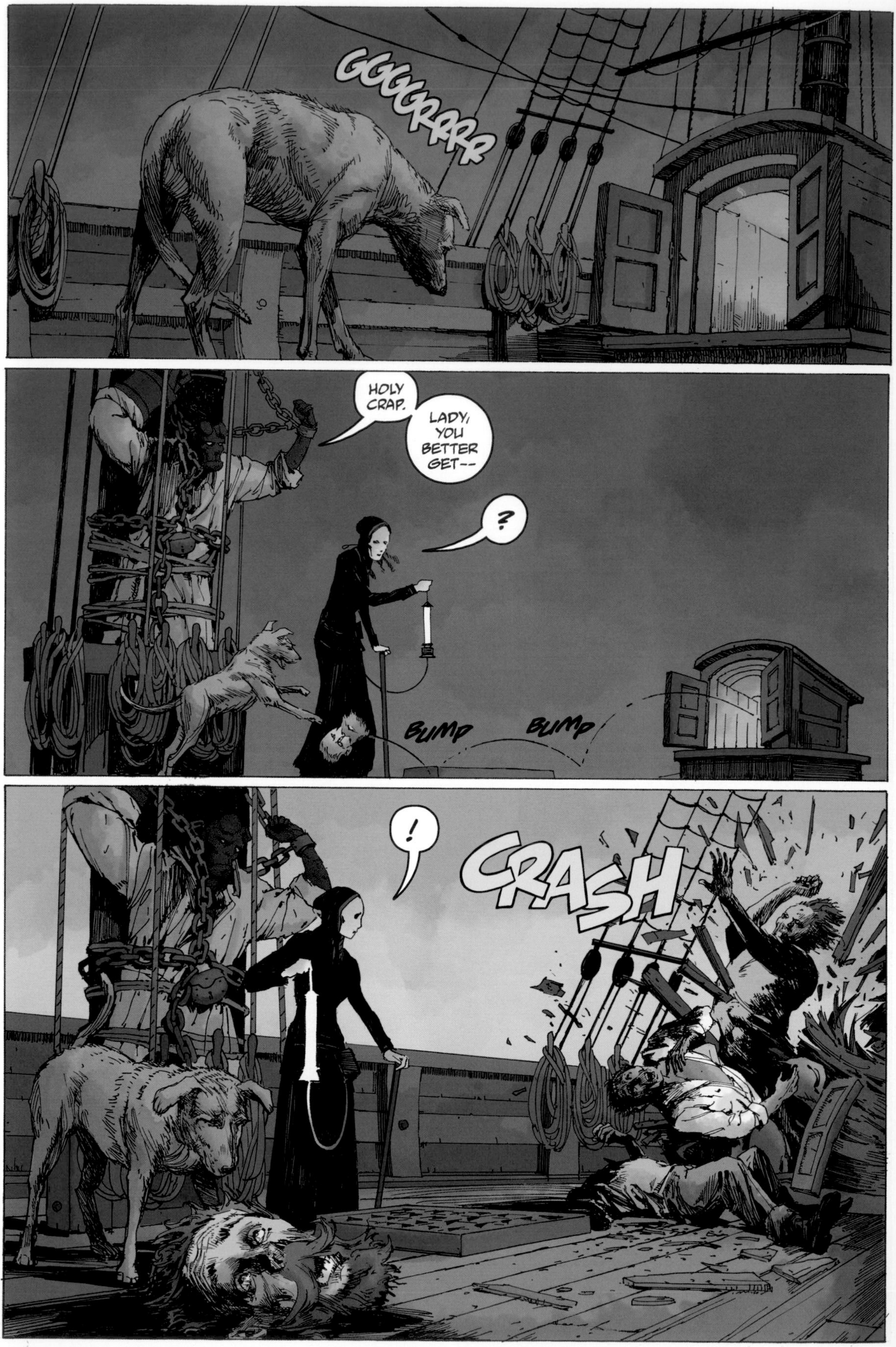
GGGGRRRRR
HOLY CRAP.
LADY, YOU BETTER GET--
?
BUMP
BUMP
!
CRASH

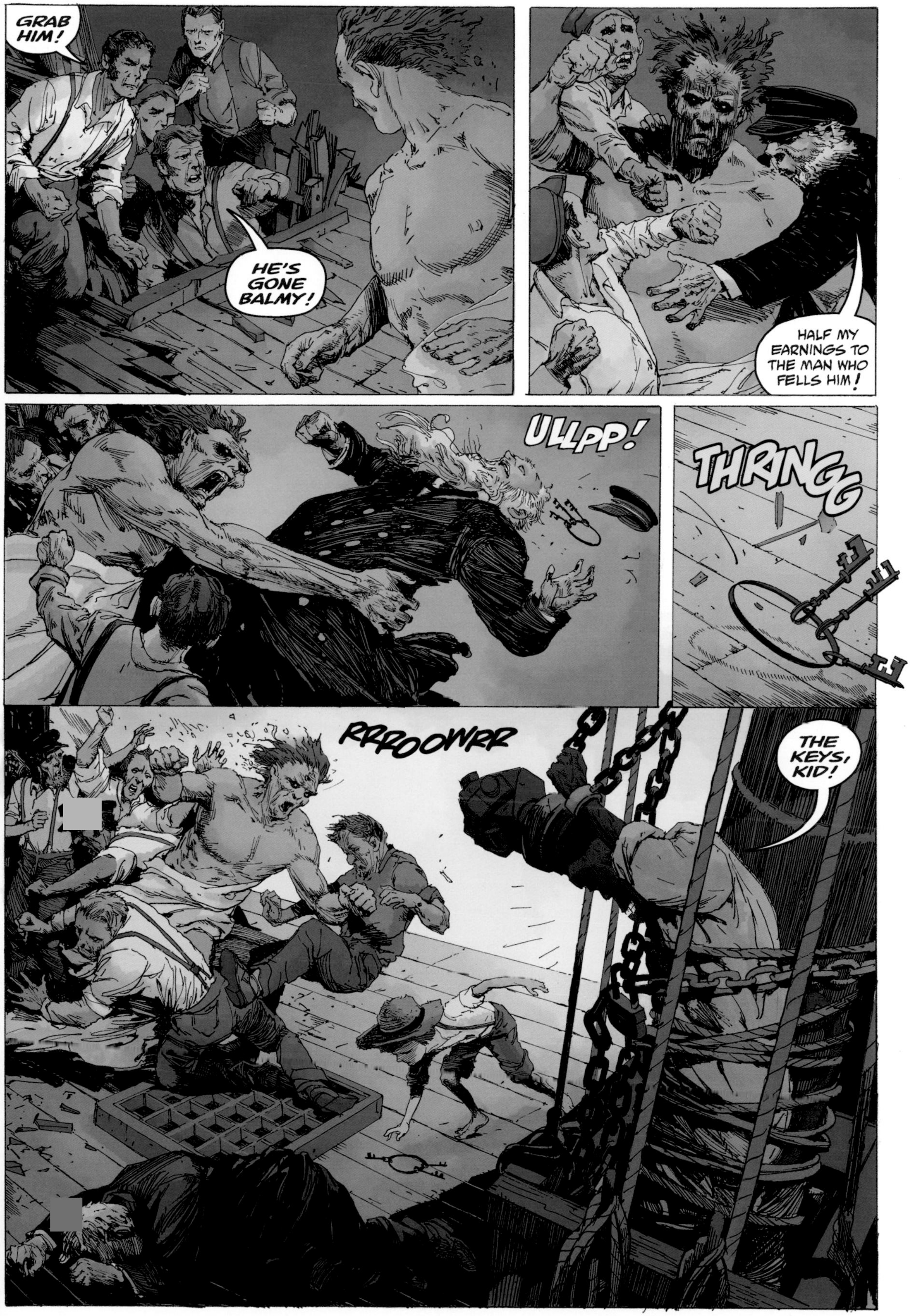
GRAB HIM!
HE'S GONE BALMY!
HALF MY EARNINGS TO THE MAN WHO FELLS HIM!
ULLPP!
THRINGG
RRROOWRR
THE KEYS, KID!

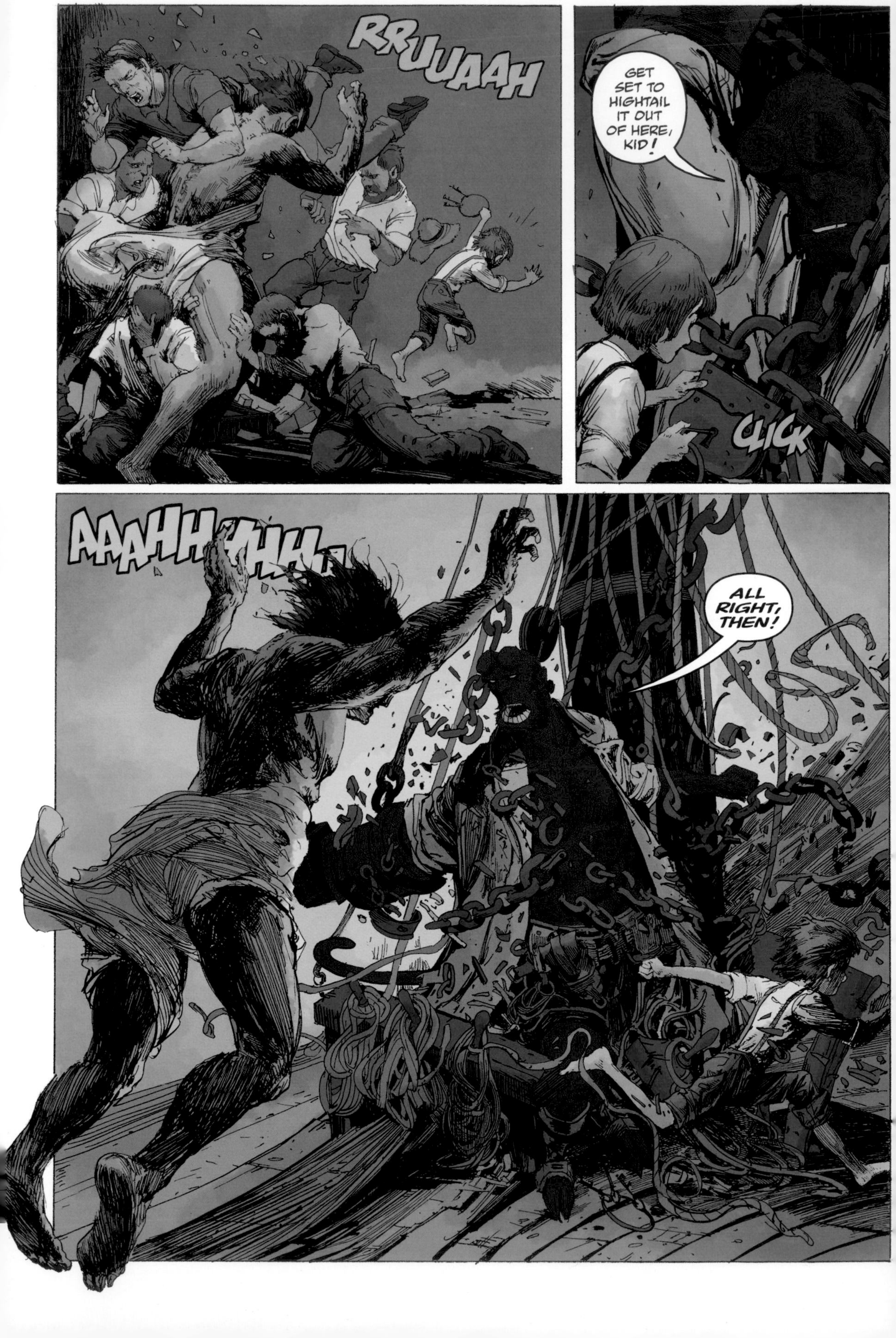
RRUUAAH
GET SET TO HIGHTAIL IT OUT OF HERE, KID!
CLICK
ALL RIGHT, THEN!

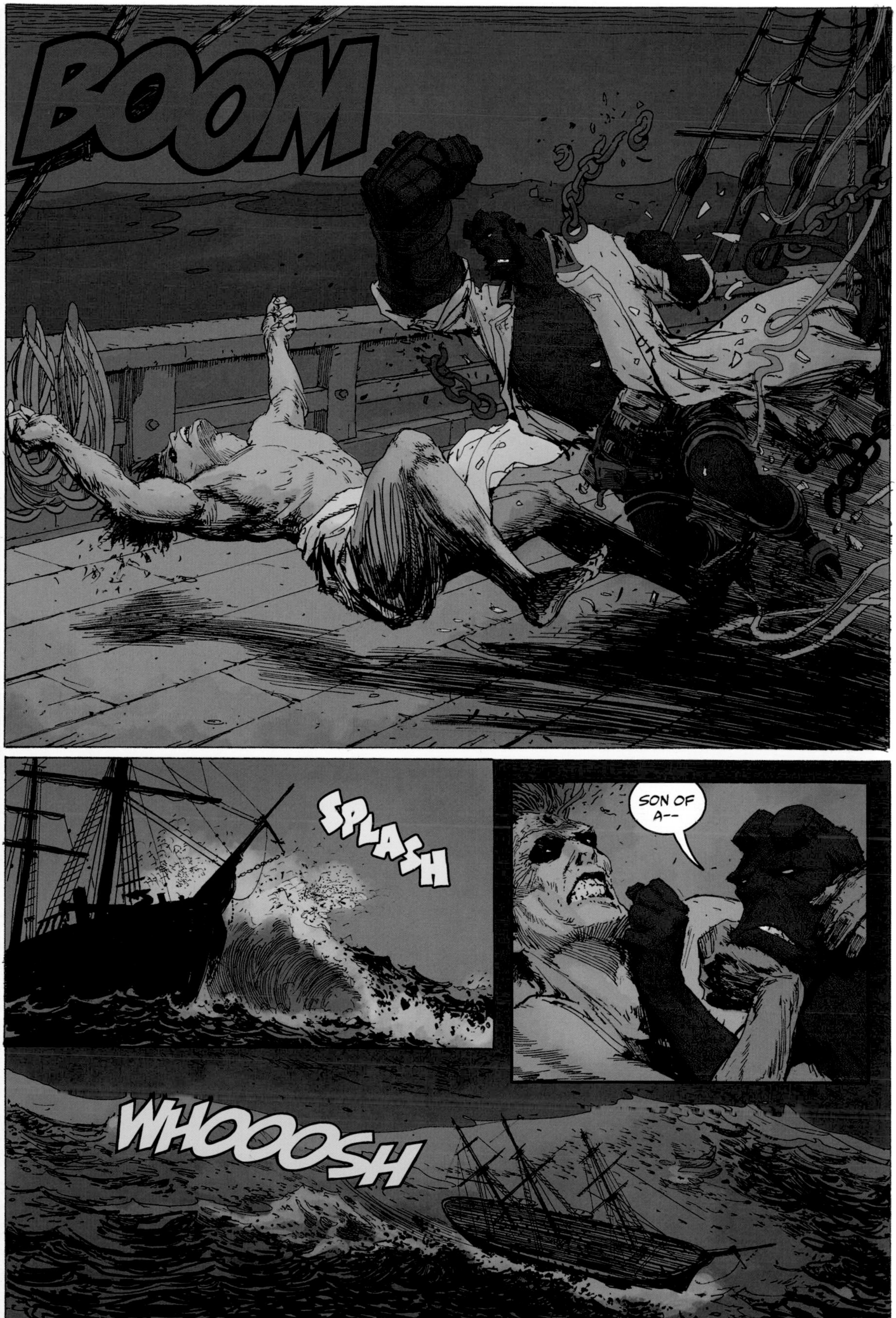
BOOM
SPLASH
SON OF A--
WHOOOSH

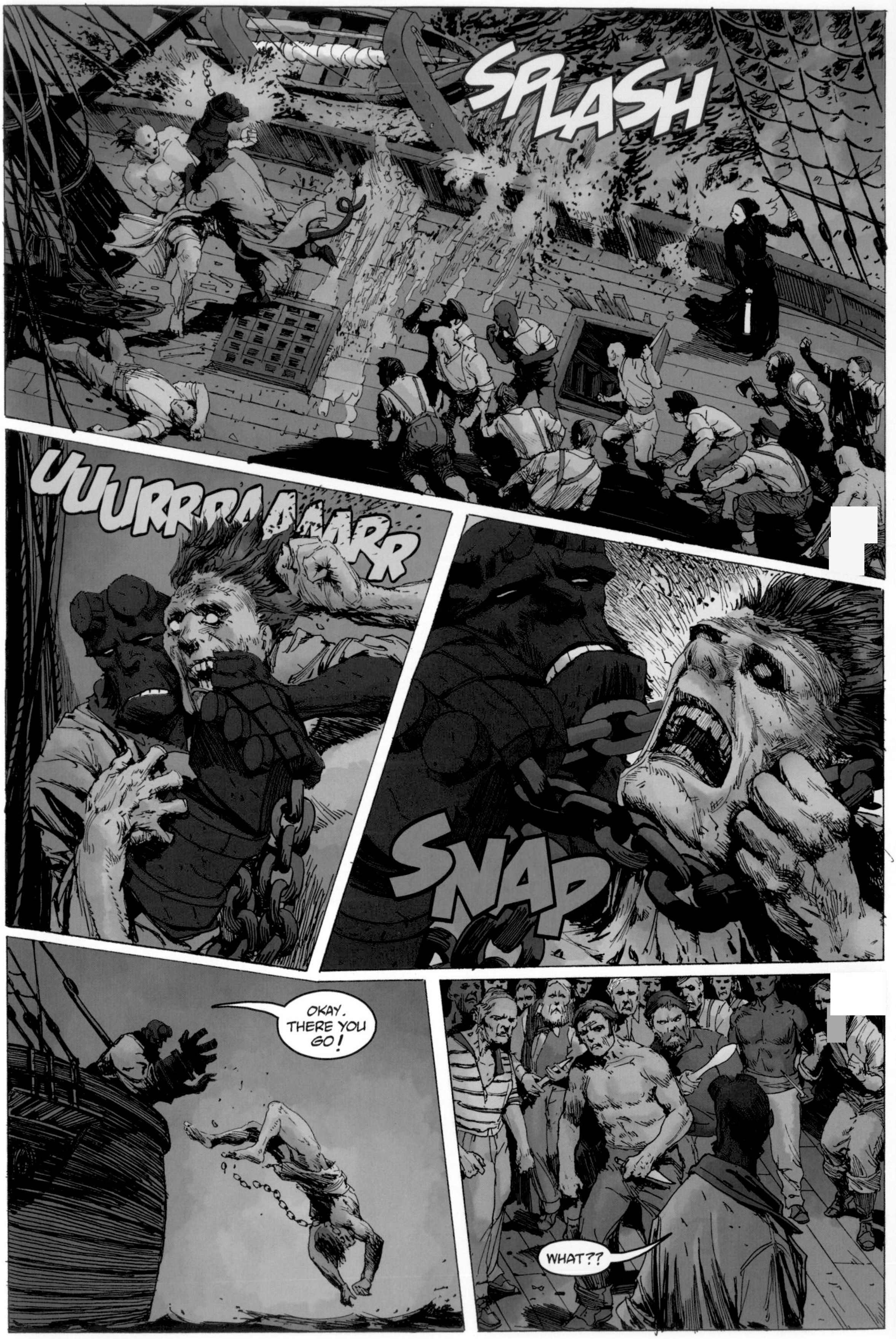
SPLASH
UUURRRAAARRR
SNAP
OKAY. THERE YOU GO!
WHAT??

YOU CAN'T BLAME 'EM FOR BEING FIDGETY, COMMODORE!

IT'S THE SORT OF DARK, BLACK NIGHT WHEN SEAMEN'S YARNS COME TRUE!

MMOOWOOWW

OOOWWOOW

HEAR THAT, CAPTAIN? SHE BECKONS!

SOMETHING HUGE, OFF TO STARBOARD!

BATTEN DOWN HATCHES--BEAR AWAY, LIVELY THERE!

PLANT THOSE SEA BOOTS INTO THE FROTH, BOYS!

SPLOOSH

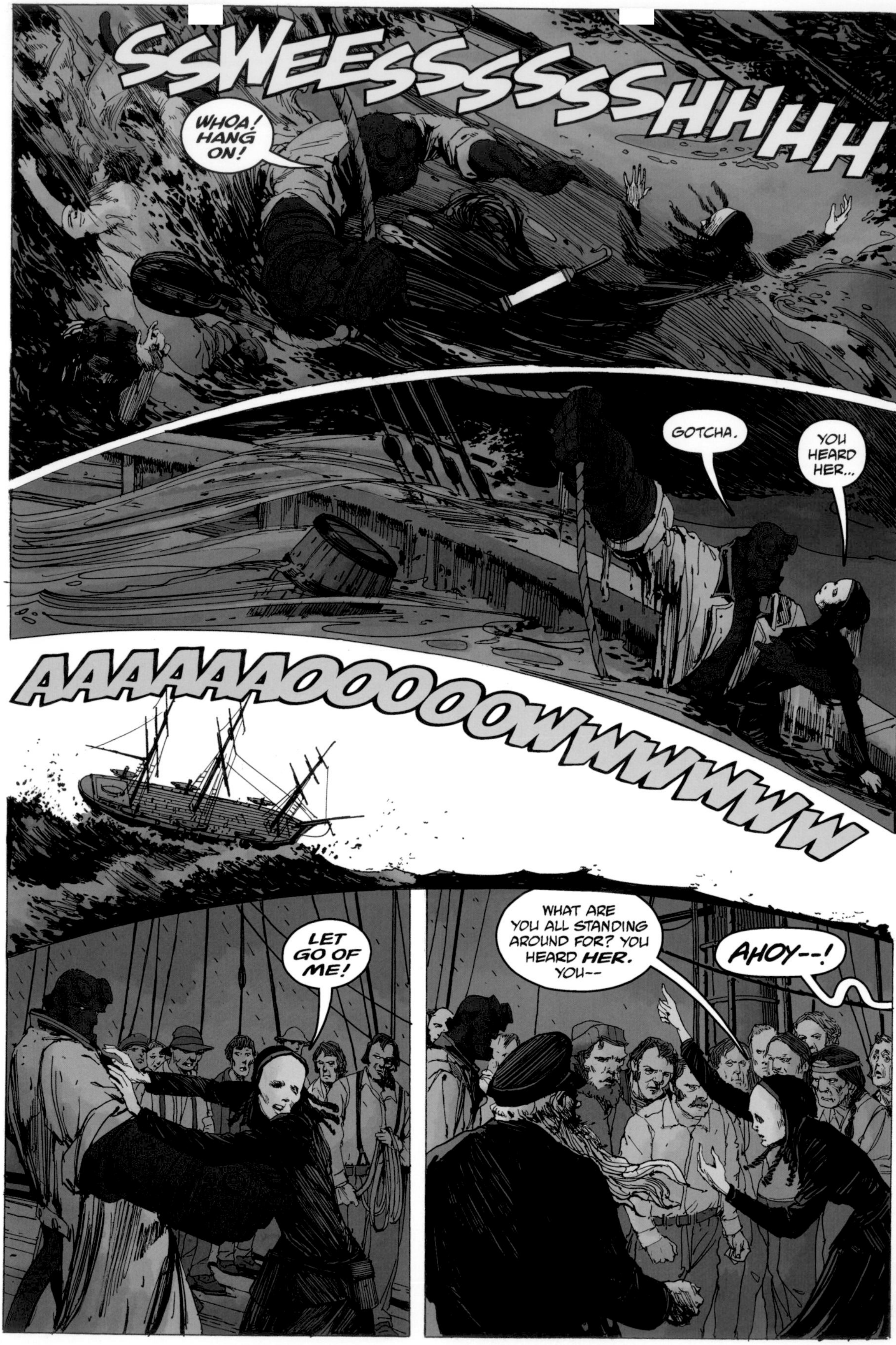
SSWEESSSSSSHHHHH
WHOA! HANG ON!
GOTCHA.
YOU HEARD HER...
AAAAAOOOOOOWWWWWWW
LET GO OF ME!
WHAT ARE YOU ALL STANDING AROUND FOR? YOU HEARD HER. YOU--
AHOY--!

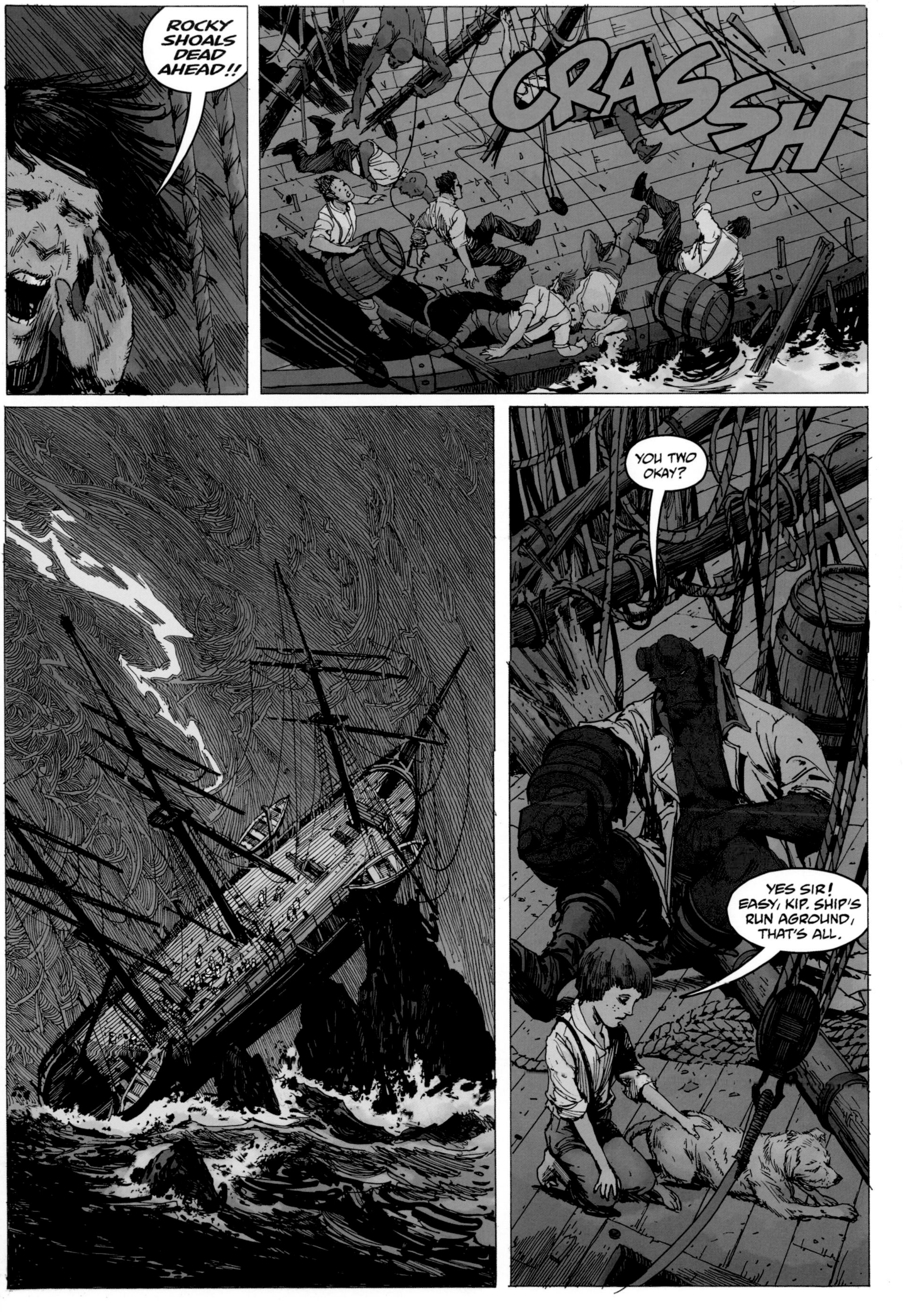
ROCKY SHOALS DEAD AHEAD!!
CRASSH
YOU TWO OKAY?
YES SIR! EASY, KIP. SHIP'S RUN AGROUND, THAT'S ALL.

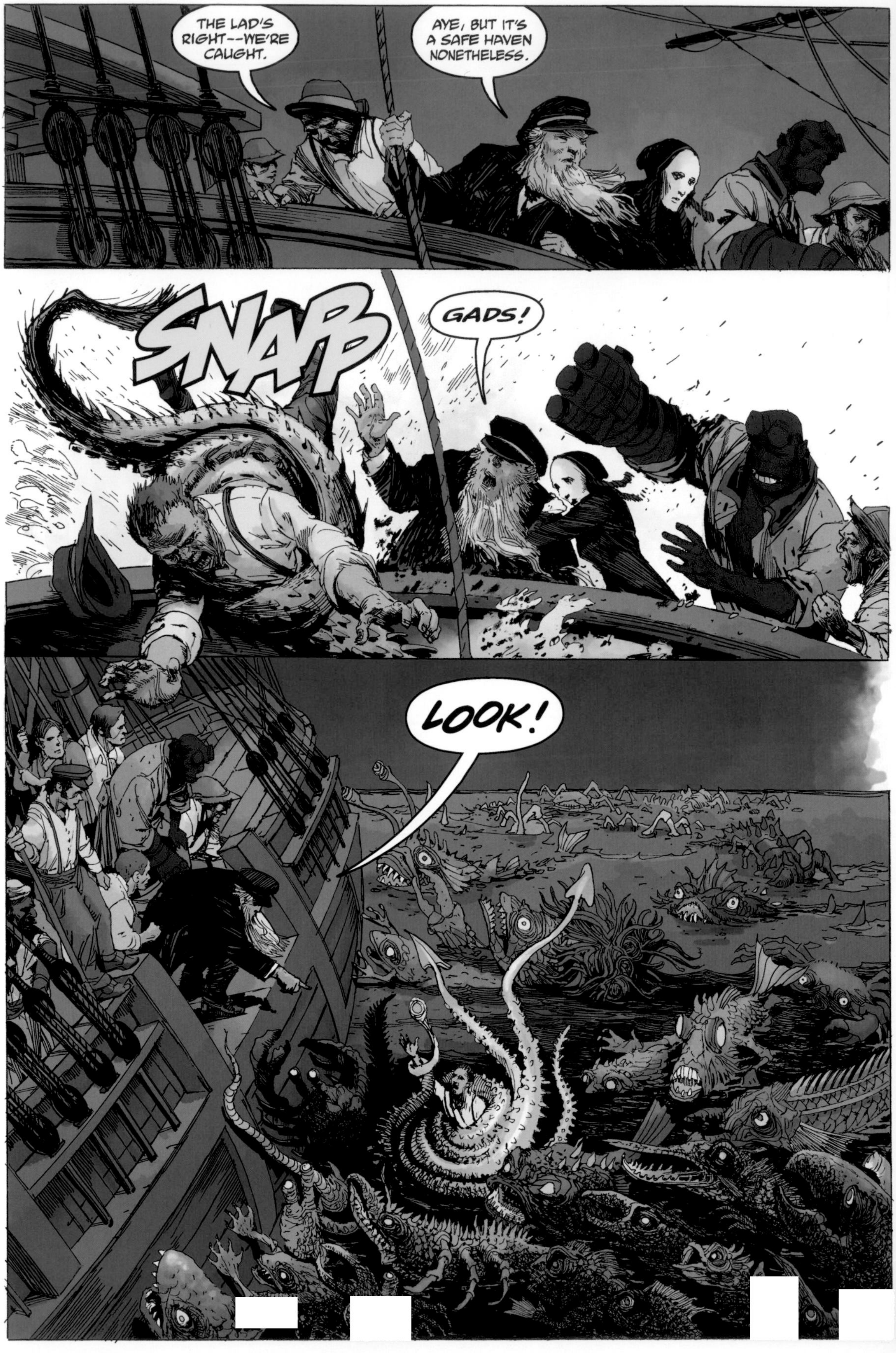
THE LAD'S RIGHT--WE'RE CAUGHT.
AYE, BUT IT'S A SAFE HAVEN NONETHELESS.
SNAP
GADS!
LOOK!

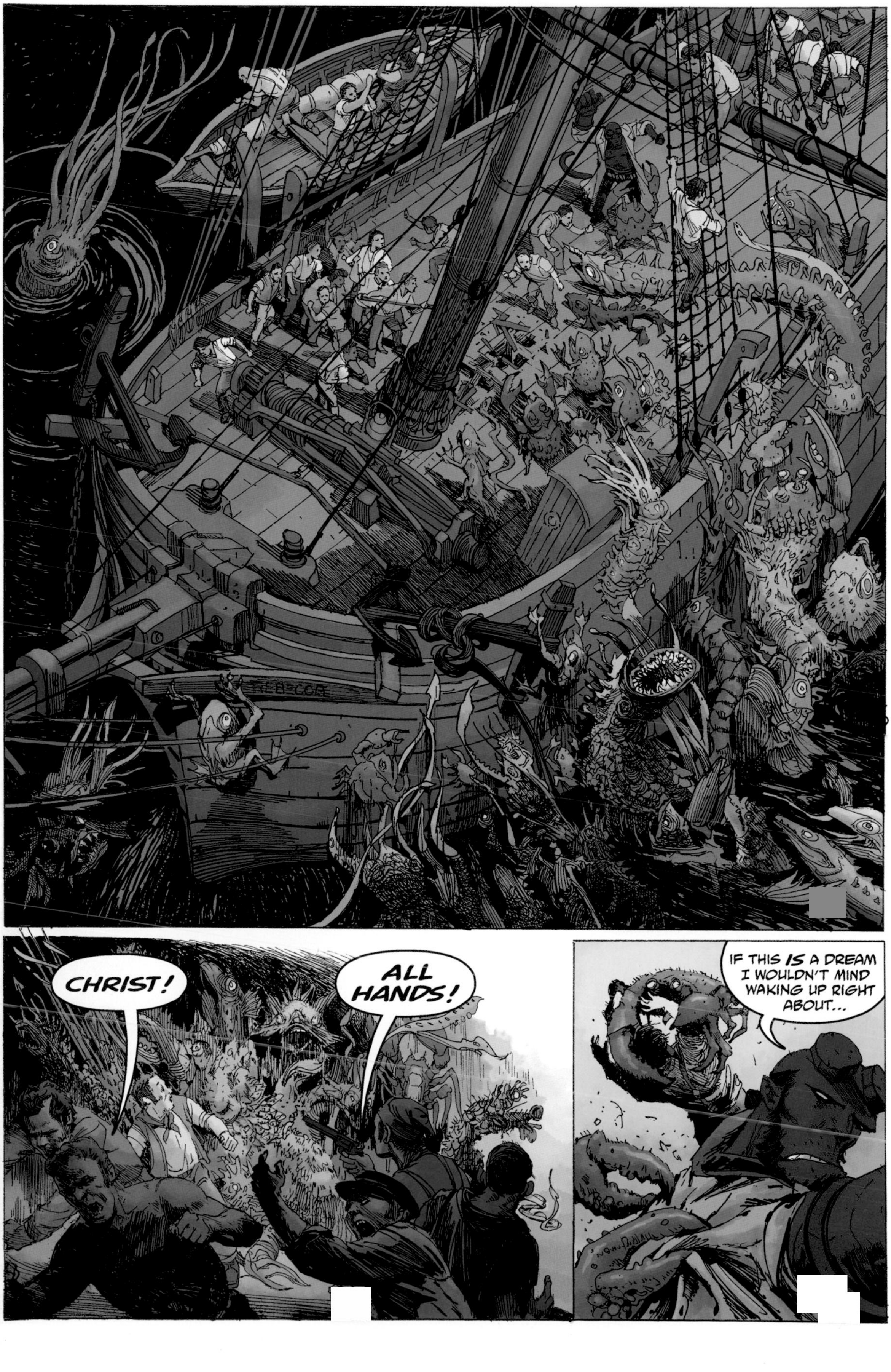
CHRIST!
ALL HANDS!
IF THIS *IS* A DREAM I WOULDN'T MIND WAKING UP RIGHT ABOUT...

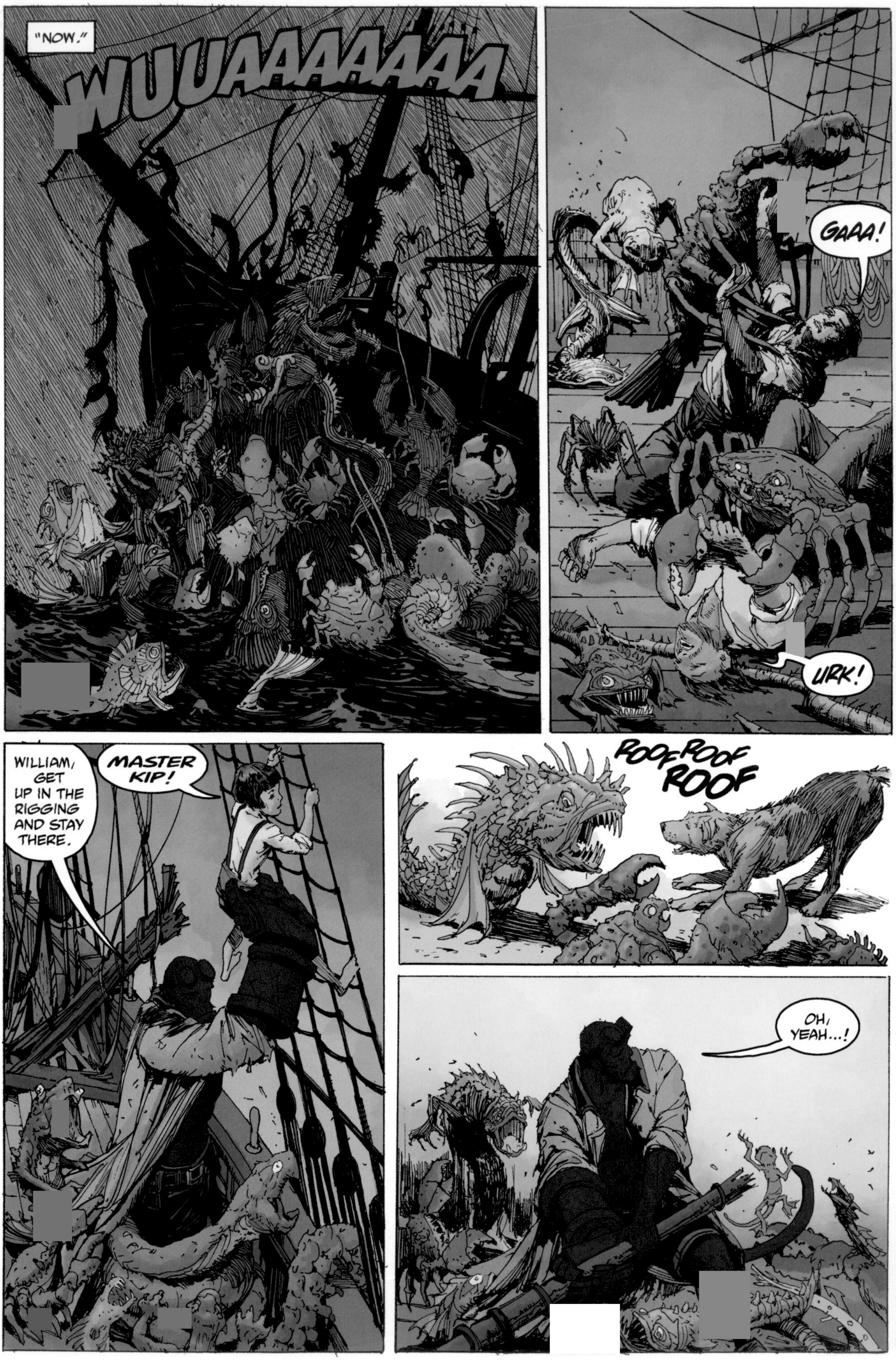
"NOW."
WUUAAAAAAAA
GAAA!
URK!
WILLIAM, GET UP IN THE RIGGING AND STAY THERE.
MASTER KIP!
ROOF ROOF ROOF
OH, YEAH...!

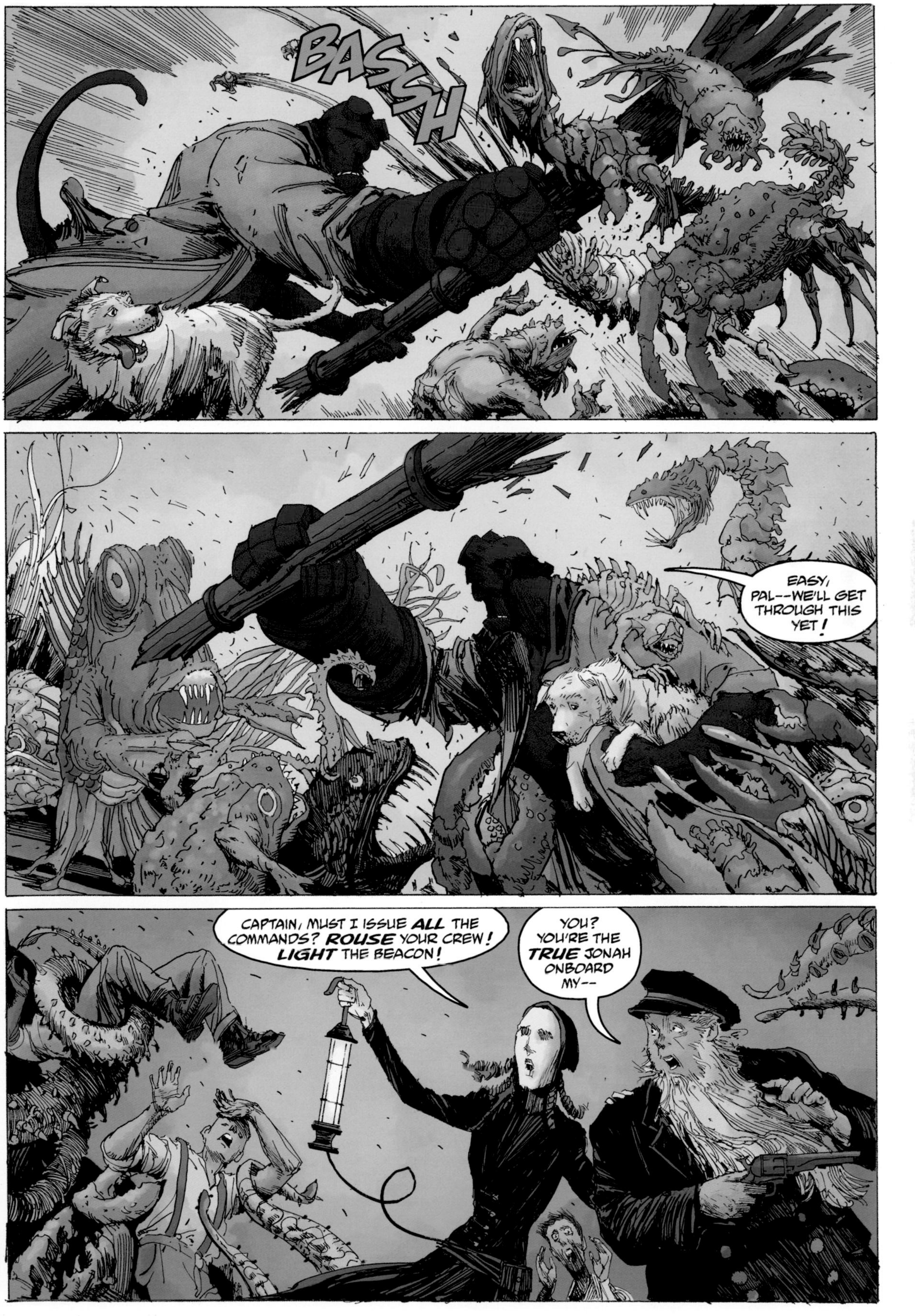
BASSSH
EASY, PAL--WE'LL GET THROUGH THIS YET!
CAPTAIN, MUST I ISSUE ALL THE COMMANDS? ROUSE YOUR CREW! LIGHT THE BEACON!
YOU? YOU'RE THE TRUE JONAH ONBOARD MY--

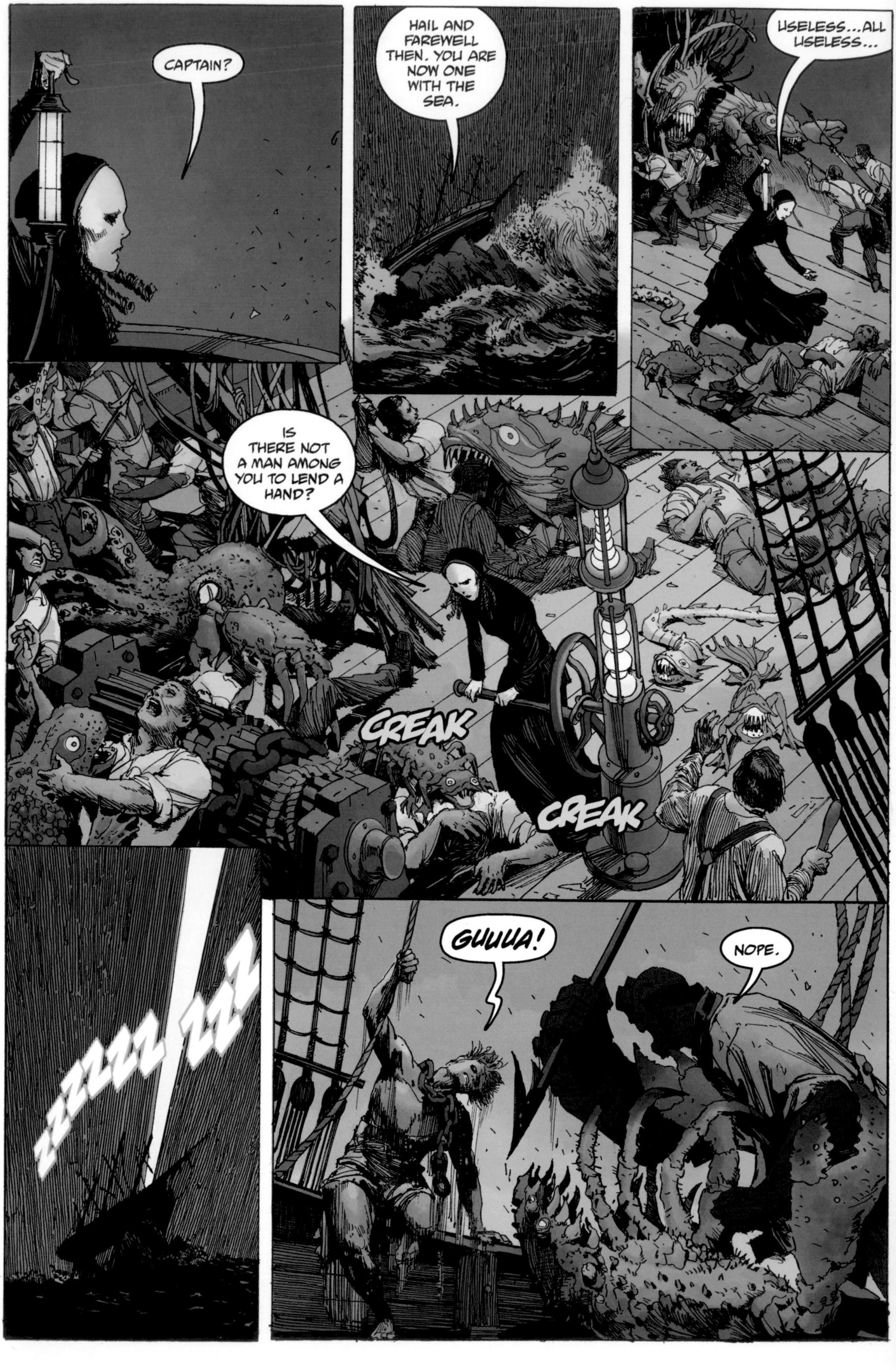
CAPTAIN?
HAIL AND FAREWELL THEN. YOU ARE NOW ONE WITH THE SEA.
USELESS...ALL USELESS...
IS THERE NOT A MAN AMONG YOU TO LEND A HAND?
CREAK
CREAK
ZZZZZZ ZZZ
GUUUA!
NOPE.

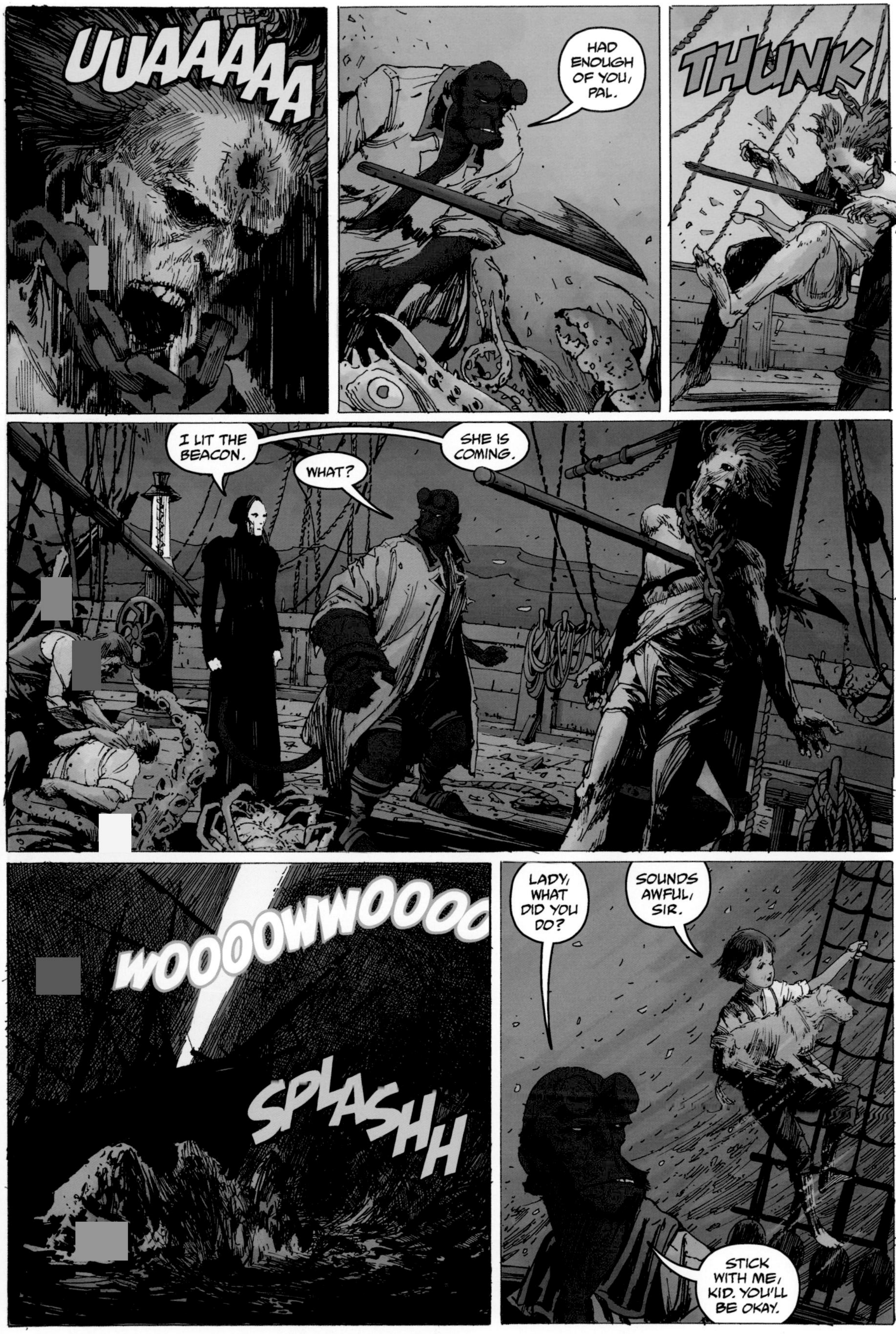
UUAAAAAA
HAD ENOUGH OF YOU, PAL.
THUNK
I LIT THE BEACON.
WHAT?
SHE IS COMING.
WOOOOWWOOOO
SPLASHH
LADY, WHAT DID YOU DO?
SOUNDS AWFUL, SIR.
STICK WITH ME, KID. YOU'LL BE OKAY.

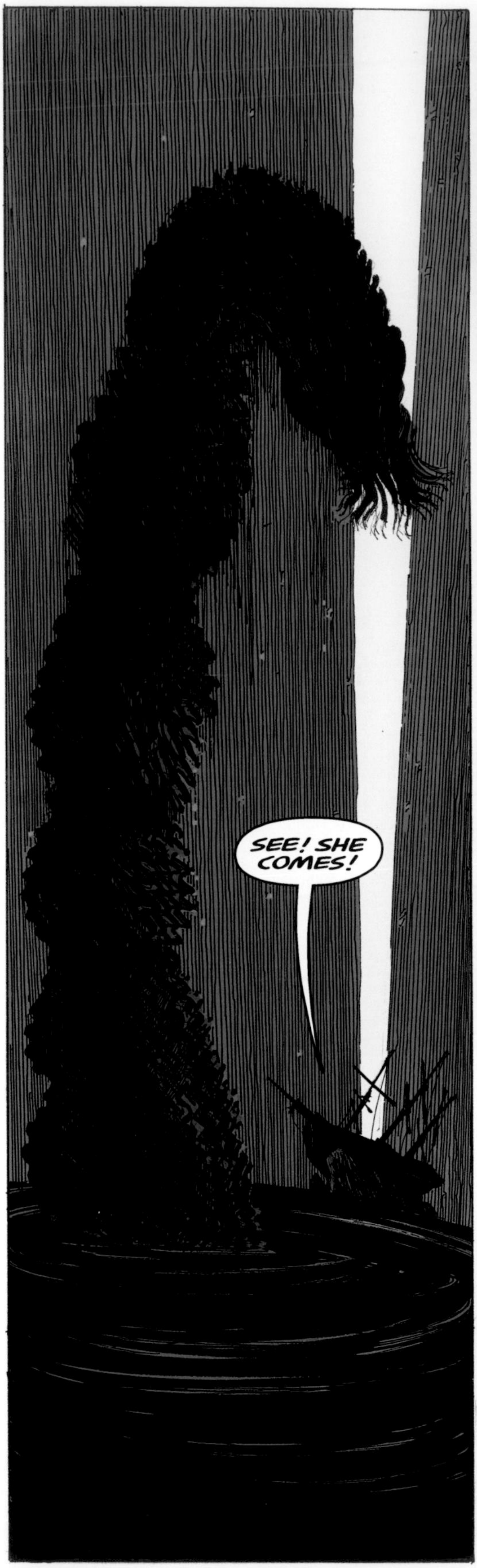
SEE! SHE COMES!

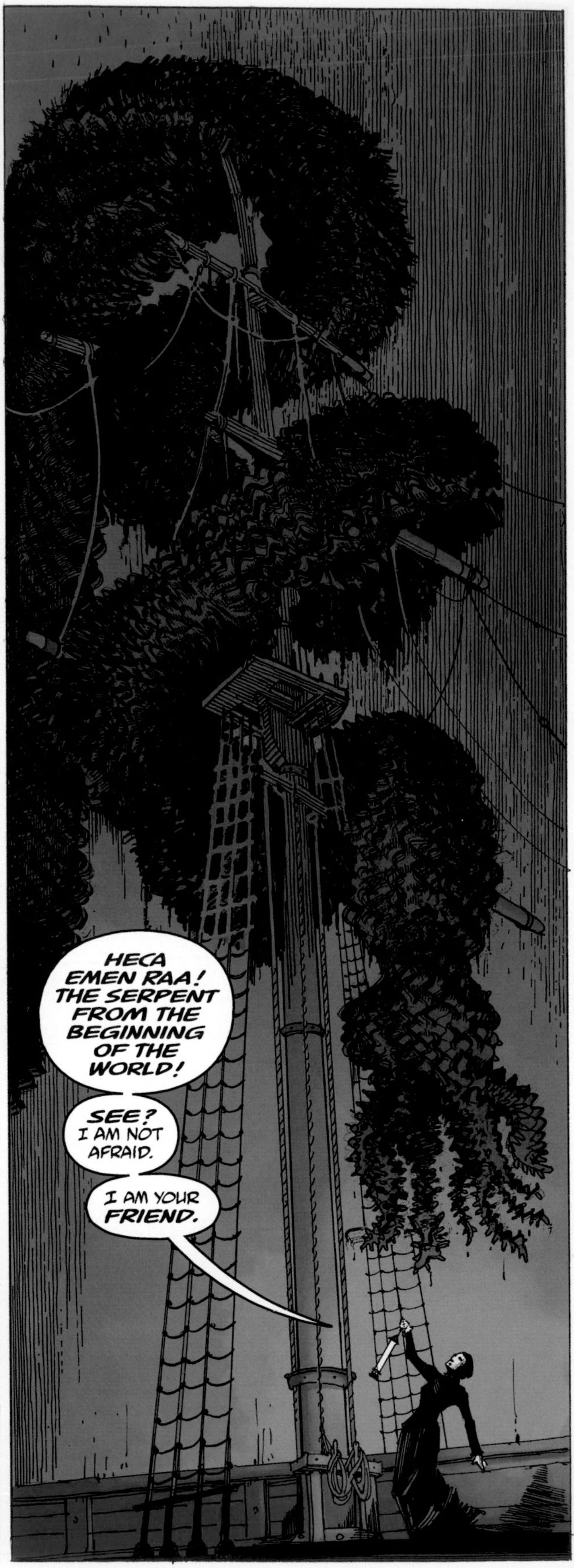
HECA EMEN RAA! THE SERPENT FROM THE BEGINNING OF THE WORLD!
SEE? I AM NOT AFRAID.
I AM YOUR FRIEND.

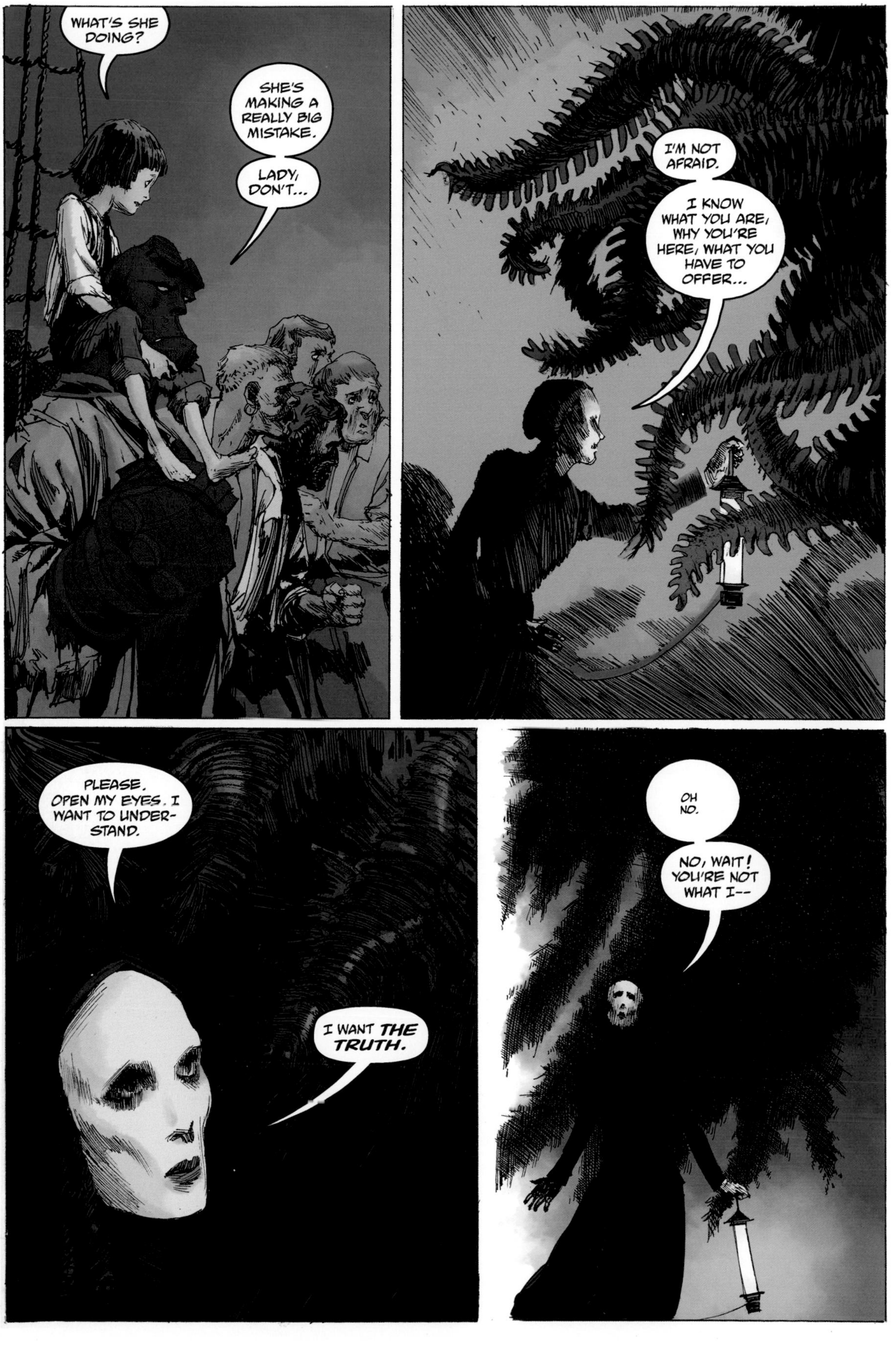
WHAT'S SHE DOING?
SHE'S MAKING A REALLY BIG MISTAKE.
LADY, DON'T...
I'M NOT AFRAID.
I KNOW WHAT YOU ARE, WHY YOU'RE HERE, WHAT YOU HAVE TO OFFER...
PLEASE. OPEN MY EYES. I WANT TO UNDER-STAND.
I WANT THE TRUTH.
OH NO.
NO, WAIT! YOU'RE NOT WHAT I--

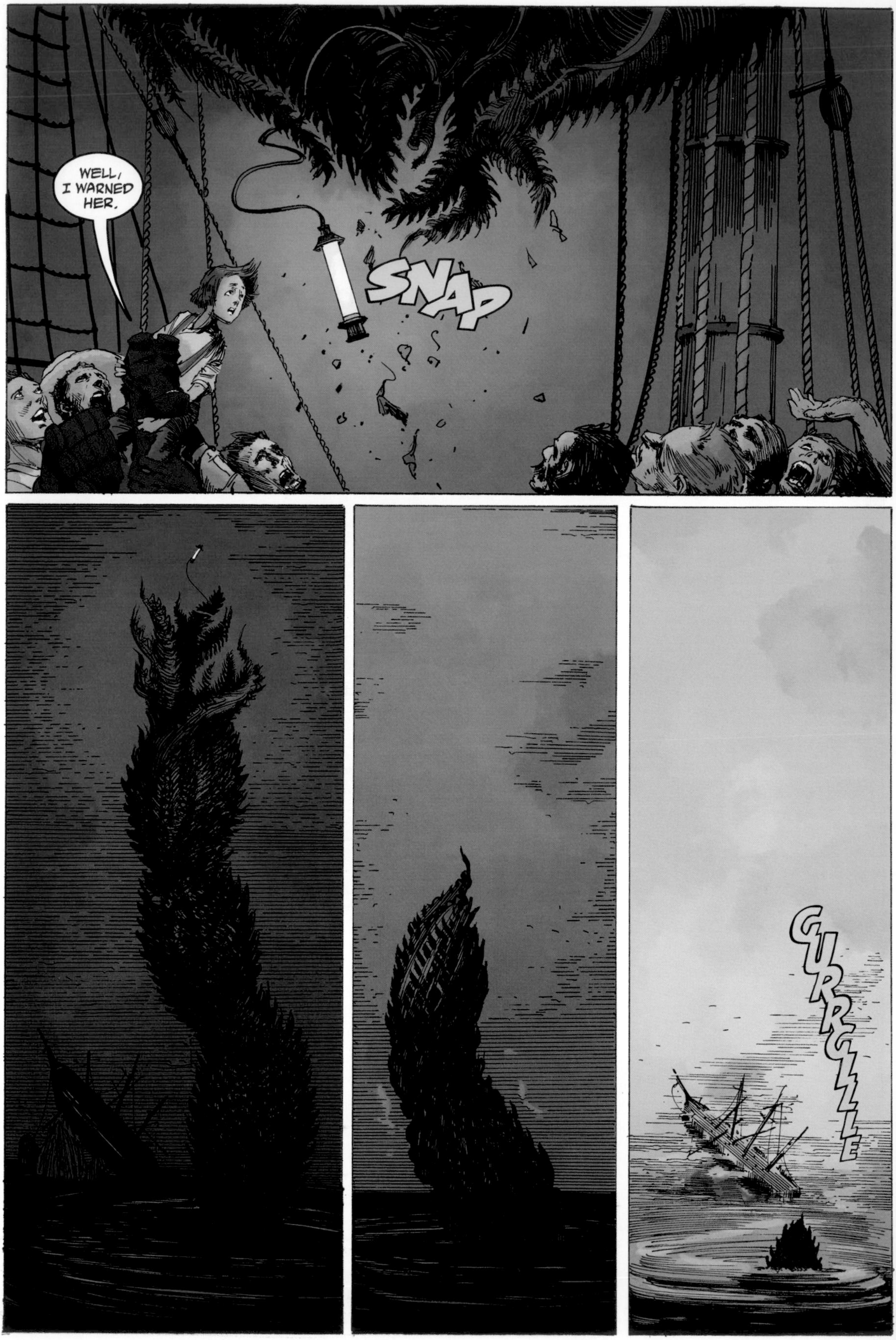
WELL, I WARNED HER.
SNAP
GURGLLE

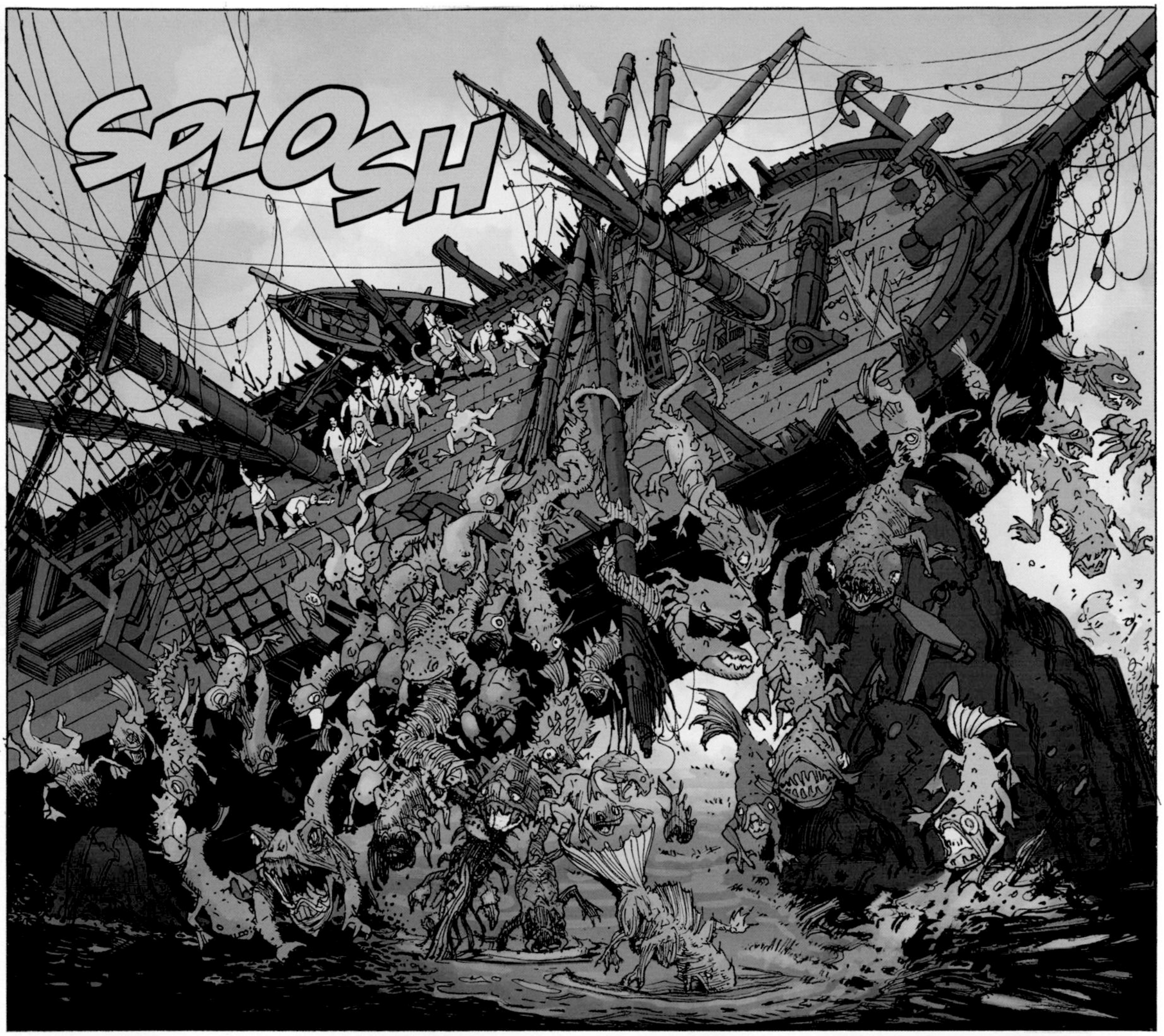
SPLOSH

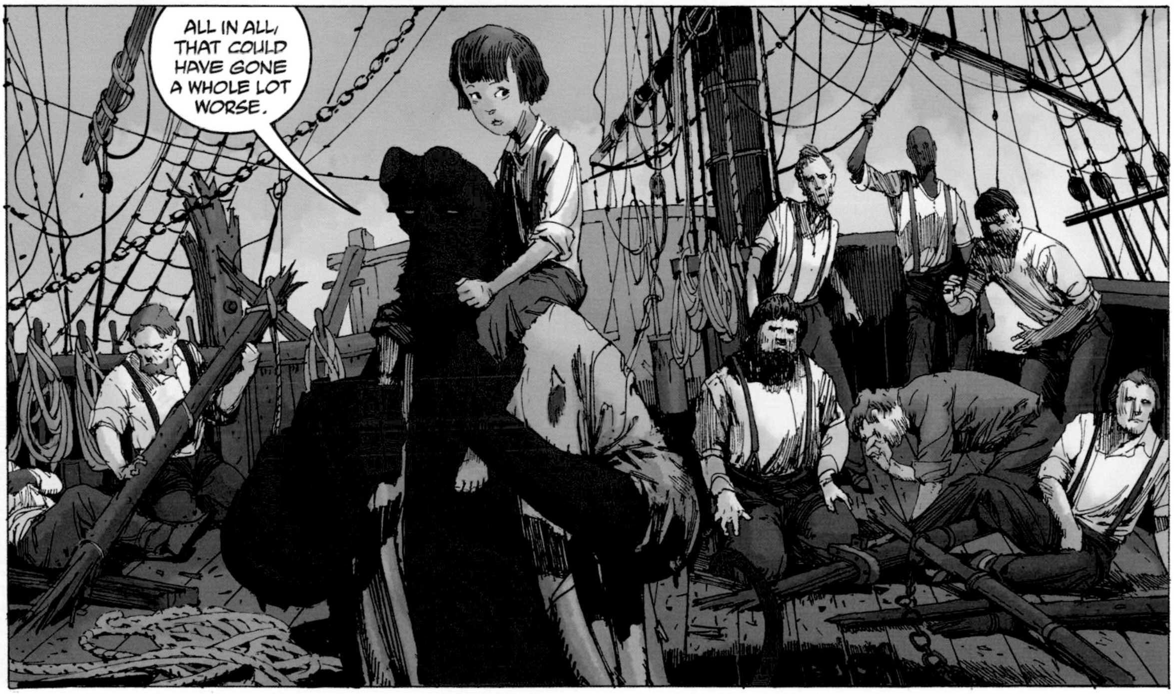
ALL IN ALL, THAT COULD HAVE GONE A WHOLE LOT WORSE.

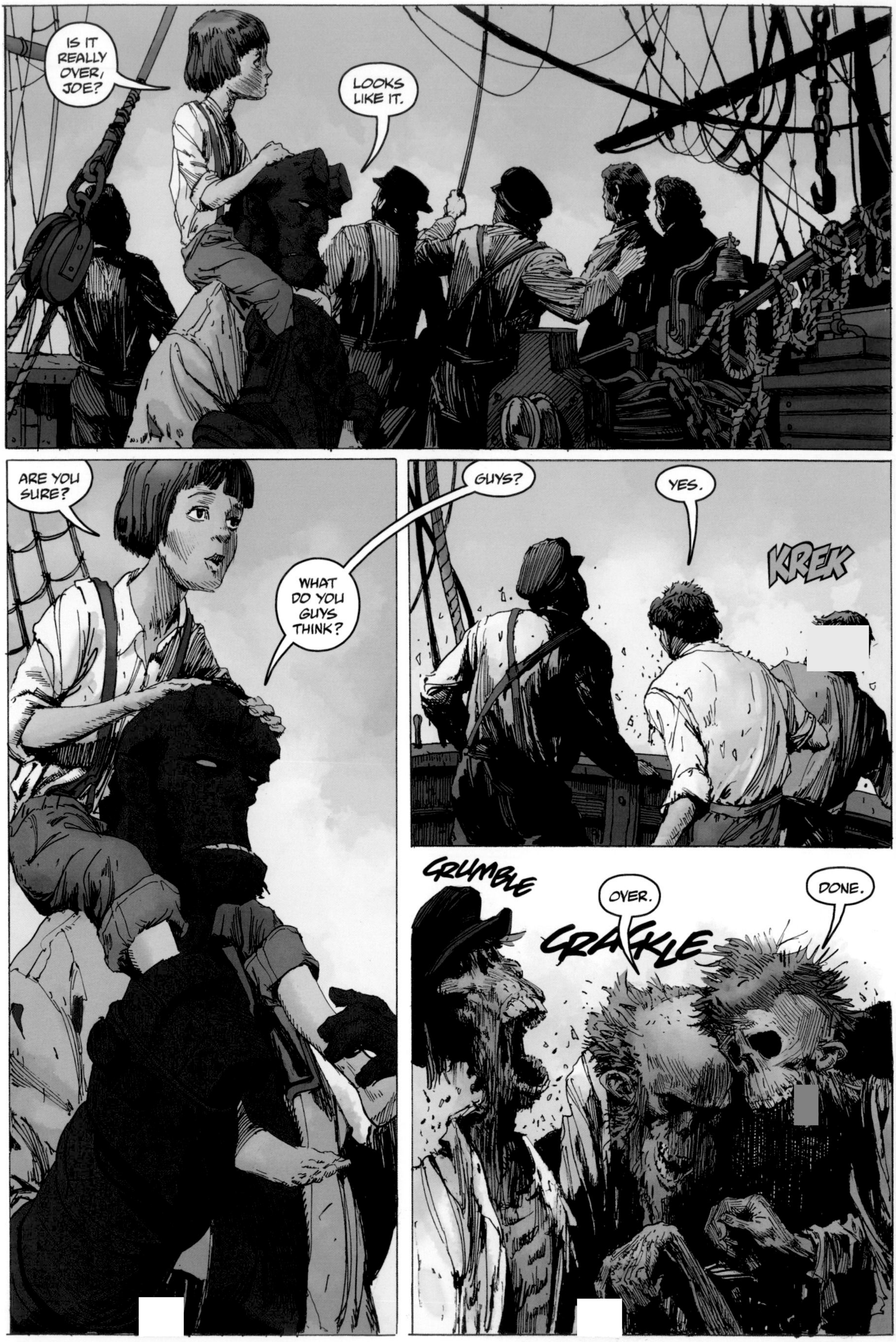
IS IT REALLY OVER, JOE?
LOOKS LIKE IT.
ARE YOU SURE?
WHAT DO YOU GUYS THINK?
GUYS?
YES.
KREK
CRUMBLE
CRACKLE
OVER.
DONE.

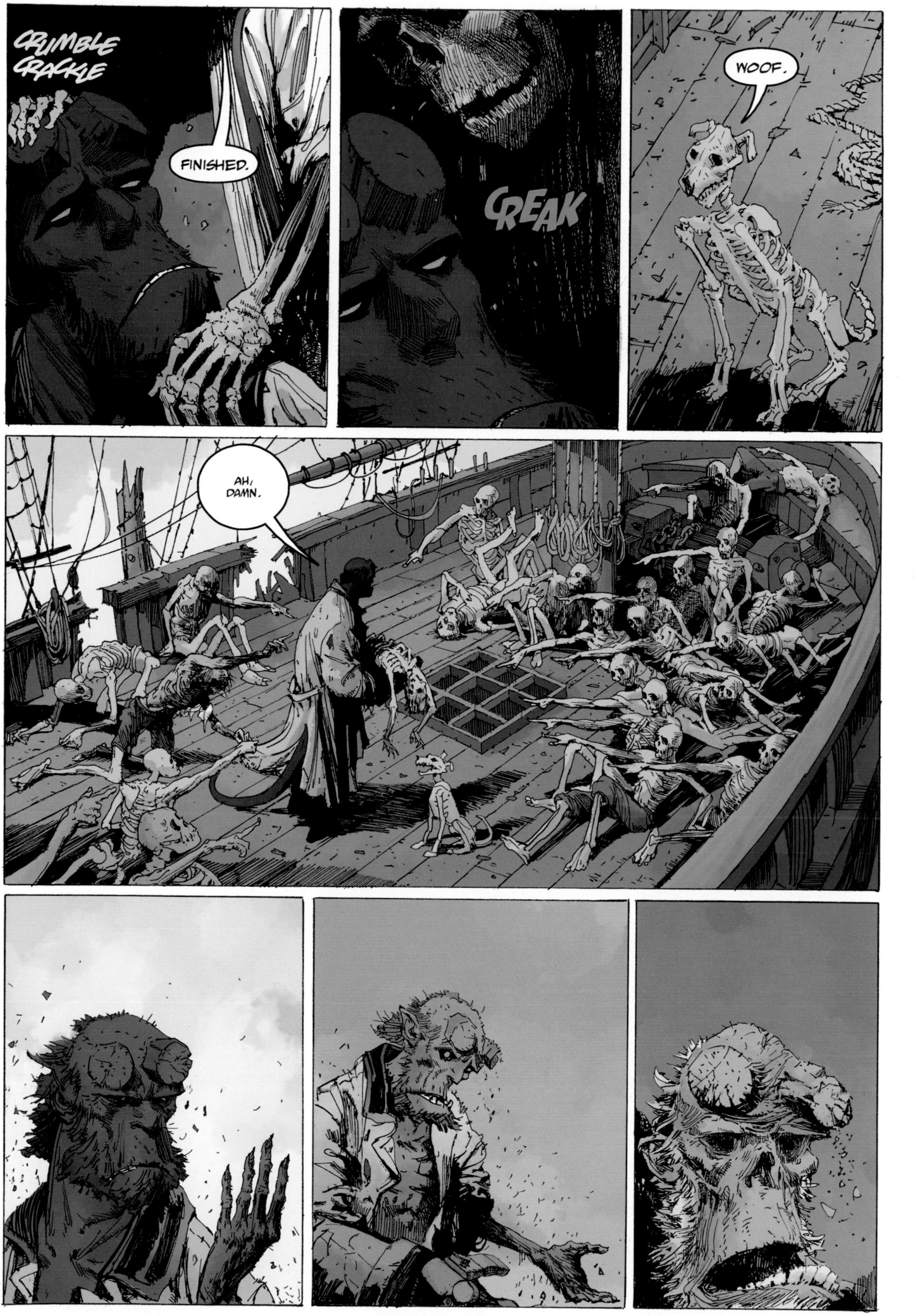
CRUMBLE
CRACKLE
FINISHED.
CREAK
WOOF.
AH, DAMN.

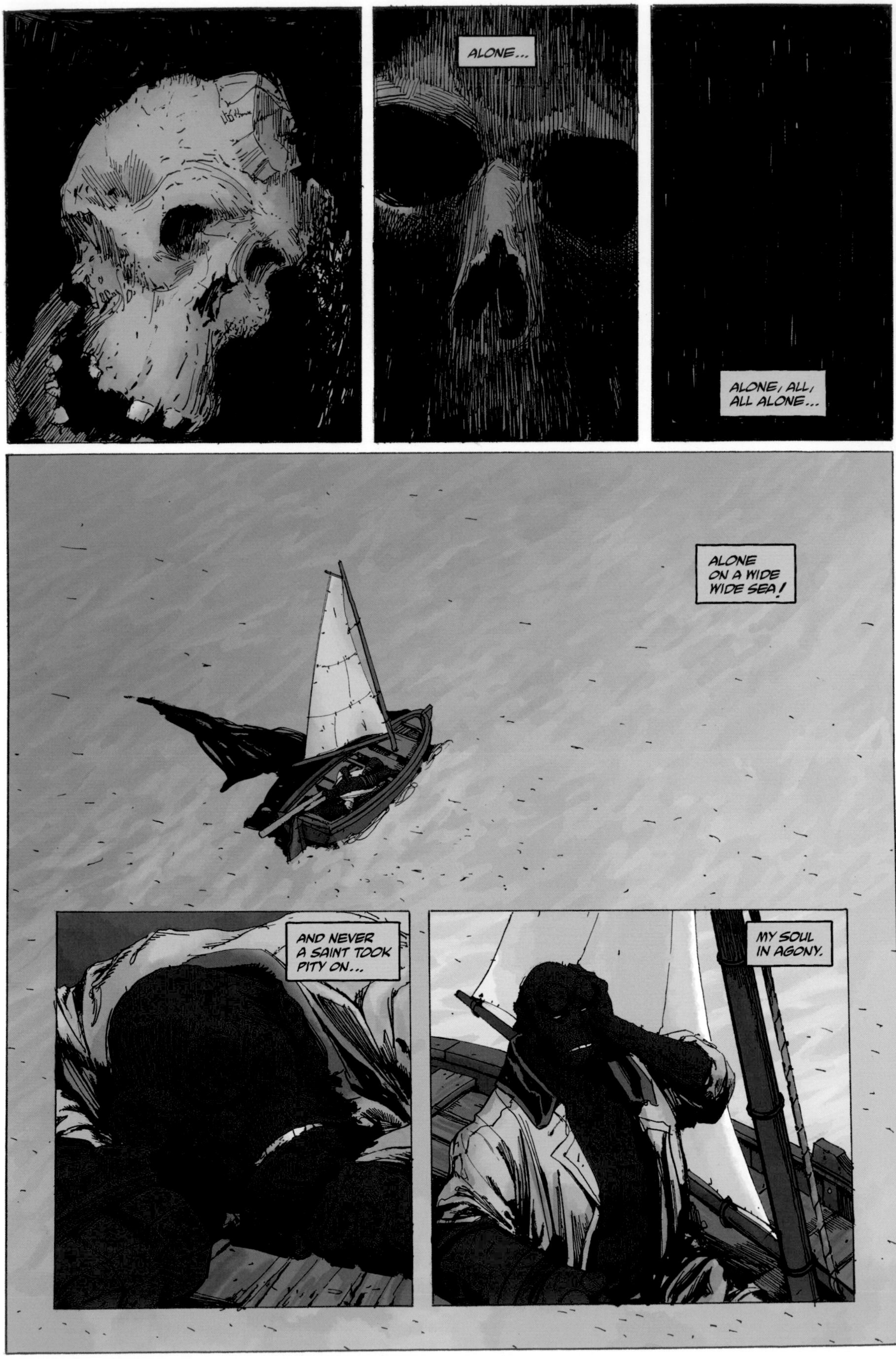
ALONE...
ALONE, ALL, ALL ALONE...
ALONE ON A WIDE WIDE SEA!
AND NEVER A SAINT TOOK PITY ON...
MY SOUL IN AGONY.

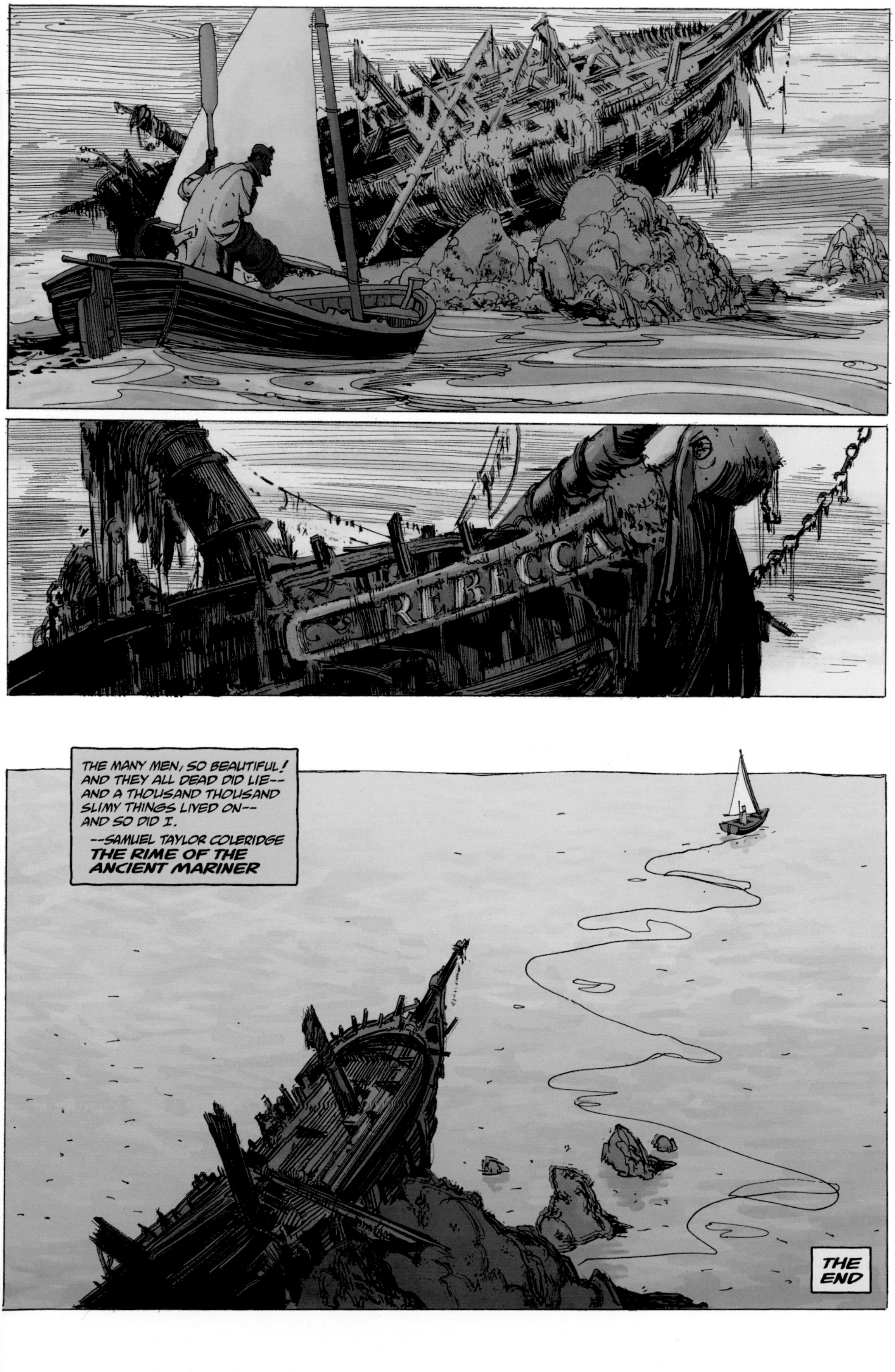
REBECCA
THE MANY MEN, SO BEAUTIFUL! AND THEY ALL DEAD DID LIE-- AND A THOUSAND THOUSAND SLIMY THINGS LIVED ON-- AND SO DID I.
--SAMUEL TAYLOR COLERIDGE
THE RIME OF THE ANCIENT MARINER
THE END

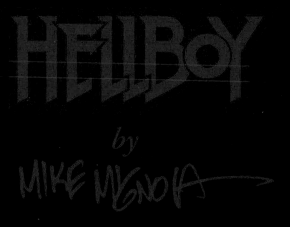

HELLBOY by MIKE MIGNOLA

HELLBOY LIBRARY
EDITION VOLUME 1:
Seed of Destruction
and Wake the Devil
ISBN 978-1-59307-910-9 | $49.99

HELLBOY LIBRARY
EDITION VOLUME 2:
The Chained Coffin
and The Right Hand of Doom
ISBN 978-1-59307-989-5 | $49.99

HELLBOY LIBRARY
EDITION VOLUME 3:
Conqueror Worm and Strange Places
ISBN 978-1-59582-352-6 | $49.99

HELLBOY LIBRARY
EDITION VOLUME 4:
The Crooked Man and
the Troll Witch
with Richard Corben and others
ISBN 978-1-59582-658-9 | $49.99

HELLBOY LIBRARY
EDITION VOLUME 5:
Darkness Calls and the Wild Hunt
with Duncan Fegredo
ISBN 978-1-59582-886-6 | $49.99

HELLBOY LIBRARY
EDITION VOLUME 6:
The Storm and the Fury
and The Bride of Hell
with Duncan Fegredo, Richard Corben,
Kevin Nowlan, and Scott Hampton
ISBN 978-1-61655-133-9 | $49.99

SEED OF DESTRUCTION
with John Byrne
ISBN 978-1-59307-094-6 | $17.99

WAKE THE DEVIL
ISBN 978-1-59307-095-3 | $17.99

THE CHAINED COFFIN
AND OTHERS
ISBN 978-1-59307-091-5 | $17.99

THE RIGHT HAND
OF DOOM
ISBN 978-1-59307-093-9 | $17.99

CONQUEROR WORM
ISBN 978-1-59307-092-2 | $17.99

STRANGE PLACES
ISBN 978-1-59307-475-3 | $17.99

THE TROLL WITCH
AND OTHERS
with Richard Corben and others
ISBN 978-1-59307-860-7 | $17.99

DARKNESS CALLS
with Duncan Fegredo
ISBN 978-1-59307-896-6 | $19.99

THE WILD HUNT
with Duncan Fegredo
ISBN 978-1-59582-431-8 | $19.99

THE CROOKED MAN AND OTHERS
with Richard Corben
ISBN 978-1-59582-477-6 | $17.99

THE BRIDE OF HELL AND OTHERS
with Richard Corben, Kevin Nowlan, and
Scott Hampton
ISBN 978-1-59582-740-1 | $19.99

THE STORM AND THE FURY
with Duncan Fegredo
ISBN 978-1-59582-827-9 | $19.99

HOUSE OF THE LIVING DEAD
with Richard Corben
ISBN 978-1-59582-757-9 | $14.99

THE MIDNIGHT CIRCUS
with Duncan Fegredo
ISBN 978-1-61655-238-1 | $14.99

INTO THE SILENT SEA
with Gary Gianni
ISBN 978-1-50670-143-1 | $14.99

HELLBOY IN MEXICO
with Richard Corben, Fábio Moon,
Gabriel Bá, and others
ISBN 978-1-61655-897-0 | $19.99

HELLBOY IN HELL
VOLUME 1: THE DESCENT
ISBN 978-1-61655-444-6 | $17.99

HELLBOY IN HELL
VOLUME 2: THE
DEATH CARD
ISBN 978-1-50670-113-4 | $17.99

HELLBOY: THE FIRST
20 YEARS
ISBN 978-1-61655-353-1 | $19.99

THE ART OF HELLBOY
ISBN 978-1-59307-089-2 | $29.99

GARY GIANNI'S MONSTERMEN
AND OTHER SCARY STORIES
By Gary Gianni
ISBN 978-1-59582-829-3 | $24.99

HELLBOY II:
THE ART OF THE MOVIE
ISBN 978-1-59307-964-2 | $24.99

HELLBOY: THE COMPANION
ISBN 978-1-59307-655-9 | $14.99

HELLBOY: WEIRD TALES
ISBN 978-1-61655-510-8 | $24.99

HELLBOY: MASKS AND MONSTERS
with James Robinson and Scott Benefiel
ISBN 978-1-59582-567-4 | $17.99

HELLBOY AND THE B.P.R.D: 1952
with John Arcudi and Alex Maleev
ISBN 978-1-61655-660-0 | $19.99

HELLBOY AND THE B.P.R.D: 1953
with Chris Roberson, Ben Stenbeck,
Paolo Rivera, and Joe Rivera
ISBN 978-1-61655-967-0 | $19.99

THE HELLBOY 100 PROJECT
TPB: ISBN 978-1-61655-932-8 | $12.99
HC: ISBN 978-1-61655-933-5 | $24.99

NOVELS

HELLBOY: EMERALD HELL
By Tom Piccirilli
ISBN 978-1-59582-141-6 | $12.99

HELLBOY: THE ALL-SEEING EYE
By Mark Morris
ISBN 978-1-59582-142-3 | $12.99

HELLBOY: THE FIRE WOLVES
By Tim Lebbon
ISBN 978-1-59582-204-8 | $12.99

HELLBOY: THE ICE WOLVES
By Mark Chadbourn
ISBN 978-1-59582-205-5 | $12.99

AVAILABLE AT YOUR LOCAL COMICS SHOP OR BOOKSTORE! • To find a comics shop in your area, call 1-888-266-4226.
For more information or to order direct visit DarkHorse.com or call 1-800-862-0052 Mon.–Fri. 9 AM to 5 PM Pacific Time.
Prices and availability subject to change without notice.

DarkHorse.com

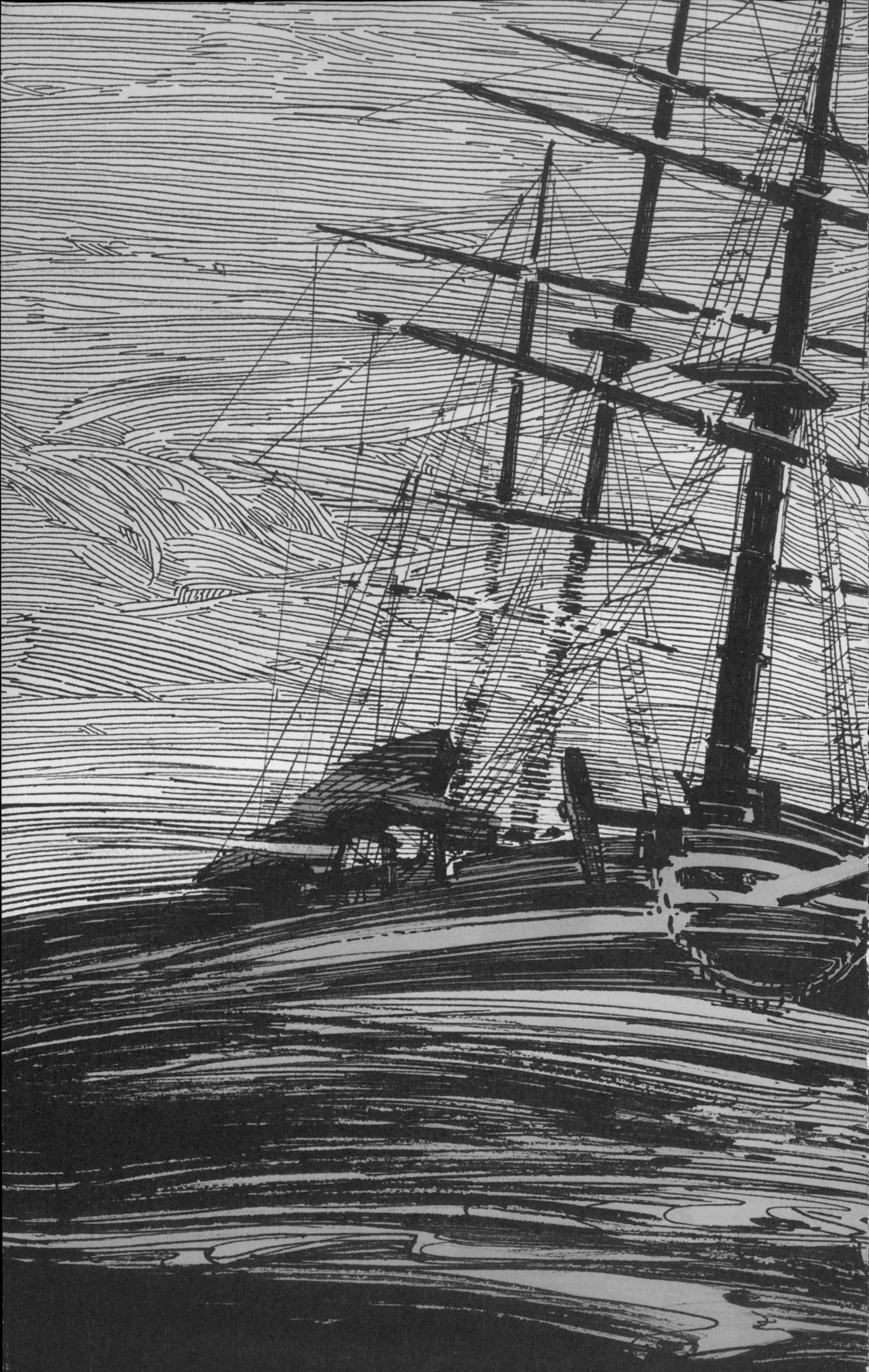